# Men of the Cave

# By

# Marisette Burgess

Tabitha,

Have fun reading!

Thanks,

Marisette B.

Men of the Cave
©2012 by Marisette Burgess

The characters and events in this book are fictitious. Any similarities to real persons, living or dead, are coincidental and not intended by the author.

All rights reserved. No part of this publication may be reproduced, stored in a retrieval system or transmitted in any form by any means electronic, mechanical, photocopying, recording or otherwise, except brief extracts for the purpose of reviews, without the permission of the publisher and copyright owner.

ISBN-13: 978-0-9838832-8-9

WRB Publishing
Palm City, FL 34990
wrb1174@att.net

## Dedication

To my mother Marta, my first fan, who always believed in my ability as a writer; and
To my husband Joshua, whose unyielding encouragement and support have gone far beyond the duties of a husband.
My Love to them Both

## Acknowledgements

I would like to extend a heart full of gratitude to all those who read Men of the Cave first, and gave their valuable advice: JB, MP, MA, ML, and TK.

I am incredibly grateful to have had the honor of meeting and working with Charlene Crandall, who's insightful advice brought life to the characters in Men of the Cave.

To my PCWW's, who's encouragement and support go without say.

And of course to Leona and Walter Bodie who make dreams come true.

Thank you all.

## Contents

| | |
|---|---|
| Prologue | 7 |
| 1. Kasey's Host Family | 11 |
| 2. Kasey's Hostile Beginnings | 25 |
| 3. Dion's Mini Cooper | 33 |
| 4. Kasey and the Villagers | 46 |
| 5. Kasey's Family | 55 |
| 6. Kasey and the Gladiators | 62 |
| 7. Dion A Monster or A Knight | 76 |
| 8. Kasey and Destiny | 94 |
| 9. Kasey and the Mermaid | 104 |
| 10. Kasey and the Brothers | 114 |
| 11. Kasey and Hercules | 129 |
| 12. Dion's Innocence | 149 |
| 13. Kasey's Gifts | 164 |
| 14. Dion's Plea | 178 |
| 15. Kasey It's Time | 188 |
| 16. Kasey and the Fire Jumping | 205 |
| 17. Dion vs. Sam | 220 |
| 18. Kasey's Spanish Christmas | 236 |

## Prologue

Pandora's bones ached. This always meant one thing; a god was near. Her stomach cramped. Cursed most of her life with this sixth sense, she ignored it. The rain poured and lighting flashed through the small cracks in the door. She wondered, is Zeus approaching? Her isolated stone cabin kept the weather at bay. She went to the fire and threw more wood onto it. The thatched roof had several leaks, so she laid out three big buckets to keep the wooden floor dry. Then the door shook with a thunderous vibration. It was strange. Humans did not come near these parts, and the gods never knocked.

"Who's there?" She yelled. She pressed her frail body against the door, knowing she could never stop anyone, human or god, from forcing their way in.

"Open, woman!" A harsh male voice answered.

Was he a god? Why would he knock? If he were a god, he would be angry if she did not open the door. She made the decision to open. The wind was forceful, and she steadied the door so it would not blow wide open. She sheltered her eyes from the wind and rain hammering her face. Due to her blurred vision, all she could make out was a giant sized figure walking past her. When she managed to shut the door, she wiped her face with her sleeve and looked upon her guest.

She gasped. Before her stood a man of goliath proportions. He wore shiny armor. The constant flow of water dripping from his garments puddled on her dry wood floor.

He removed his helmet, then shook his long blonde hair. Two strong white feathered wings extended out from his back. He shuddered like an animal shaking its wet fur, and water sprayed in all directions.

"By the gods of Olympia, who are you? What are you?" Pandora asked.

"Gabriel is the name I was given. I am a messenger of the one true God," he said in a low gruff voice.

"The rumors around Olympia are true then?" she asked.

"I am here to find where your allegiance lies, Pandora. Will you proclaim your loyalty to the one God and do his bidding, or do you bow and kiss the feet of the gods and goddesses on Olympia?" He commanded.

The woman lowered her head and thought for a minute.

"I have been nothing more than a pawn to the gods of Olympia. Used, tricked, and lied to. I hold no allegiance to them. But why should I anger the Olympic gods by doing the will of yours?" She straightened her back and raised her chin.

"It is you who holds the key we need. If you refuse me now, the immortal life Zeus has granted you will end here. If you aid my God, he will give you a place in the heavens where you belong."

Her shoulders sagged, her chin lowered, she stared at the angel before her. "If it is truth you speak and I will be granted peace in the heavens, then I will do His bidding."

"You have made a wise choice Pandora. Here is what is to come. You must stay hidden and away from the Olympic gods until the battle is over. You will be vital to the preservation of humanity, but it will not come to pass for a long time. Do you still hold the jar created by Zeus?" The angel asked.

"I do. It is hidden within the depths of my heart." Pandora placed her pale fist over her heart. "It only contains hope for I already let out all the evil into the world."

"That is well enough. You must preserve that jar at all costs. It is crucial to our success. Do you understand?" The angel affirmed.

"I do," Pandora reassured him.

"Before I go I must do one more thing. You have lived as an immortal under the rule of the pagan gods.

"Her eyes grew wide.

"Bow before me."

Pandora hesitated. He needed her, she knew he would not harm her. She fell to her knees. Gabriel stepped forward, brushed her curly strawberry hair out of her eyes, and placed his thumb on her forehead.

"Now you serve the one God. You are bound to The Almighty." With his thumb, he made a T shape on her skin.

"It will not come to pass for more than three thousand years, until a red headed female carries your blood line. Remember, protect the jar."

His wings swung forward covering his body and then he vanished.

# 1. Kasey's Host Family

Three Thousand Years Later

Balling my fists, I embraced the pain of my nails digging into my palms. The sensation a much better distraction from the torture I was about to undergo. I held my breath and clenched my jaw. Please don't vomit, I thought. Then the drop came. I felt the slight jolt from the wheels, and I let out a slow breath. The plane landed. To refocus, I blinked several times. The old woman next to me looked horrified.

"*Estas bien?*" she asked.

I had spent the last two months trying to complete as many online Spanish lessons as I could. I wanted to be prepared for my adventure in Spain. According to the program, I picked up the Spanish language very well.

"*Si, gracias,*" I replied. Embarrassed, I stood and turned to get off the death machine as quickly as they would allow me.

The busy San Sant Airport was just a blur as I tried to get through it. My stomach twisted and churned with knots. I knew he did this to me. Teal's miserable words of despair and pathetic groveling, before I boarded, were like a repeating record in my head.

Did I act too irrational when I signed up for this study abroad project last March? But who would pass up a scholarship like this one? If we were still together, would I have left for Spain? More nervous and guilty than excited, I began to doubt my decision. Was leaving the country to get away from my ex my best option?

I re-focused and concentrated on getting a cab to Deia. When I walked through the automatic doors and the hot air hit my body, I was disappointed the weather felt like back home. Then I realized the immediate landscape. A green mountain hid behind a city that blended modern day skyscrapers with old Mediterranean stoned structures. Cars honked, people yelled, a city full of energy. The traffic of people everywhere disappeared into the natural beauty all around. The contrast between gray city surrounded by vibrant greens, browns, and blues, left me breathless. No such place could exist in America. The sea salt tickled my nose, but my lungs welcomed the pure air of the island of Mallorca, Spain.

"Taxi?" The sound of a voice jerked me out of my trance.

"Uh, *si*," I answered.

He hailed a cab. After one attempt, a white car with a yellow and black stripe down the sides and on the hood pulled up. A balding man with an enormous grin exited the cab.

"*Hola soy Renaldo. Adonde vas?*" he asked speaking loud and slow. It appeared he greeted others like me before, foreign.

## Men of the Cave

Renaldo approached my bags. Once he came around the car, I saw that he was short and stocky.

"*Vas pueblo Deia*," I said with confidence.

He chuckled, "Do not worry I speak English."

He grabbed my green suitcase, the carry-on off my shoulder, and put them in the trunk. I climbed into the back of the cab. The grey interior smelled of a lovely jasmine scent. A blue beaded rosary hung from the rearview mirror. Taped to the dashboard was a wallet-sized picture of Jesus.

As Renaldo entered the cab, he asked in his broken English and heavy accent, "*Adrez in Deia?*"

I snickered at his attempt at English.

"I'm going to the Caracoles Restaurant," I answered.

"Ah, *el Restaurante Caracoles*, great food. Wonderful family. You must eat the swordfish. Very good."

"Do you know the family?" I questioned, my curiosity intensifying for any information on the family I would soon be living with for the next ten months.

"Yes, very good people." He pressed his foot to the gas pedal and accelerated out the airport at an alarming speed. His driving was fast and unpredictable. I scrambled to find the seat belt.

"No seat belts?" I panicked.

"No, they broke so I took them out. No worries, I safest driver. Never an *accidente*." He punched the gas and laughed.

As he came inches from other cars, people, and street light posts, I gripped the handle above the door, and swallowed hard the bile rising from the pit of my stomach. I shut my eyes.

"No worries, we get there by lunch, one hour or less trip."

Once we left the city, it became easier to open my eyes for seconds at a time. I gathered in as much of the scenery as possible. The man's dreadful driving made me nauseous. I wished I'd taken my motion sickness pills. How was I supposed to know that I would need them on the ground? There were fewer cars on the road once we left the city but he continued with his erratic speed. A few times, I snuck some peeks. The land's orchard of olive trees grew wild and took over the landscape. The trip seemed to take no time, because of this man's crazy driving.

"This is Deia," he exclaimed.

I pried one of my eyes open as I felt the car slowing. Once we reached a reasonable speed, I opened my eyes fully for the first time since I entered the taxicab. It was as if we were driving into a painting.

"Is it real?" I gawked.

He laughed, "Very much so, very magical she is not?"

"To say the least."

The road curved in an elongated S toward the main street. Within the swirly landscape stood the most adorable sandstone structures hiding in the luscious green of the terrain. It was almost as if the little tiled structures played peek-a-boo from behind the greenery of the over-grown land. The village began in the valley of Serra de Tramuntana between two mountainous cliffs. The ancient town seemed perfectly placed. It started in the valley, worked its way up on the side of the mountain, and finished on the rocky cliffs.

# Men of the Cave

"*El Restaurante Caracoles* just around the corner," Renaldo pointed to a bend in the road where it took a sharp right turn.

Compared to Palma, this village appeared empty. A handful of elderly villagers walked the streets. Cars parked on the sides of the street, but my taxi was the only one in motion.

As soon as we turned, I saw a blue awning hanging over a set of wicker chairs and tables. Above the blue canopy, a white sign in cursive, "*EL CARACOLE.*"

A handful of people ate at the outside tables. The first floor of the building was obviously the restaurant part. The building extended one floor above the restaurant. I guessed the Castillo family must live on the second floor. The International Language School organized my two-semester stay here in Deia, as well as my living situation.

My heart thumped when the cab stopped in front of the restaurant. I realized I only spoke twice to *Señor* Castillo. As Renaldo slammed the trunk, I exited the cab. He set my luggage next to my feet. I smoothed out my blue and brown floral skirt.

The scent of exotic spices and foods stirred my stomach. I realized I was starving. I decided that for the next ten months I would let my vegetarian preferences off the hook and enjoy dishes of all kinds.

Beyond the outdoor dining area, a long open room held round tables with white tablecloths. Large metallic rustic fans hung from the ceiling blowing massive amounts of air. The open restaurant had no air conditioning system.

On the back wall, a brown polished swinging door with a big porthole window led to the kitchen. A mural covered the walls of the entire restaurant. It matched the look of the landscape outside with not nearly the exquisiteness or color scheme of the real landscape. The ambiance from inside the restaurant was loud.

A man walked toward us from the back of the restaurant. Tall and slender with slick, black hair and a full black beard, he looked to be near his forties. He must be *Señor* Castillo since he wore an apron over his white and khaki attire.

As the man stepped from under the awning, he smiled, "Kassandra Reese I assume."

"It's a pleasure to meet you *Señor* Castillo," I said. "Call me Kasey."

"*Vale*, please call me Fernando. I hope you had a good trip, *si*?"

"Yes, thank you."

"Come, let us meet the family. I will take care of this." He pulled out his wallet and paid Renaldo. "We would have picked you up ourselves, but with the restaurant, it is very difficult. My apologies," he said overly theatrical with his gestures.

"No problem," I said.

"*Que lo pases bien muñeca*," Renaldo called. He got into his cab and sped off.

I glanced to Fernando and shrugged my shoulders. I did not understand.

"He said have a good time. He called you a doll."

"How strange, thank you," I said.

Fernando extended his hand toward the inside of the restaurant. I followed his gesture. I met some gazes from his customers, they turned away avoiding my glances. They too dramatized their expressions and mannerisms.

"You will be an attraction for the people of this village," *Señor* Castillo said. He also noticed his customers looking at me.

"What do you mean attraction?"

"Hmmm, not too many young American ladies in this village. The gentleman called you a doll because you look like a porcelain doll, and that is unusual here."

I smiled and glimpsed down at my brown sandals over my pale feet, "Thank you *señor*."

It felt awkward being the foreigner. Here in Spain, I'm the one with the unusual sexy accent. Perhaps I should dye my red hair black.

"You will be very popular. Call me Fernando, please."

We walked through the restaurant, a few customers glimpsed my way. A table of five young guys in their early teens to twenties definitely stole glances. They didn't seem Spaniard like the other locals eating at the restaurant. Their complexions had a deeper hue. When we reached the back of the room, the rest of the family came through the swinging door.

First out was a lovely and simple looking woman. She was fair and her warm smile made me feel like she should be offering me a fresh warm cookie. Behind her, three kids followed in by the order of their birth. The girl wasn't too far off from my age. She was the spitting image of her mother, fair skinned with light brown hair. The two boys didn't look like brothers at all. The youngest had his mother's pale complexion and a little of both parents in his facial features. The middle brother looked exactly like Fernando.

"Beatriz, Catalina, Garcia, Rodrigo," Fernando pointed to each person in order as he introduced them. "I would like you to meet Kasey."

I smiled trying to emulate the warmth that came from Beatriz. "*Mucho gusto*, It's finally a pleasure to meet you."

"The pleasure is all ours," Beatriz said in her heavy accent. She gave me a bear hug and kissed my cheek. She gave her daughter a look as if expecting her to do the same. The girl seemed less enthusiastic about the embrace required of her. She lowered her gaze and with a straight face kissed both my cheeks but there was no hug. The boys followed their sister with some indifference.

"Garcia, Rodrigo, please take her things up to her room," Beatriz said to her sons.

"*Vale, Mama. Podemos ir a la playa despues.* I will take Rodrigo with me," Garcia replied to his mother. My Spanish was good enough that I understood he wanted to go to the beach.

Beatriz smiled at me, "We told them they could not go until they met you. They have been waiting all day." She turned to Rodrigo, "Si."

Both boys kissed their parents on the cheek, grabbed my things, and ran back through the swinging kitchen door.

"I will be upstairs on the computer, *vale*," Catalina sulked. She left without giving her parents a kiss.

"Forgive us for her less than acceptable hospitality," Beatriz looked concerned as if I were a judge.

"She is a difficult seventeen year-old," Fernando added.

"She is a strong personality," Beatriz corrected.

I smiled and changed the awkward subject, "I'm amazed that everyone speaks English and so well too."

"We must. With the island's big tourist population it is to our advantage to know a few key languages. The children go to a multilingual school, Spanish, English, and French. Beatriz and I are well versed in English and French as well. I could defend myself fairly well with Italian, Portuguese, and German," Fernando informed me.

"That's amazing. My Spanish isn't nearly that good. I'll need your help practicing."

"Of course, here, let me introduce you to some of the *clientele*." Fernando headed for the outside dining area.

Beatriz interrupted, "She must be hungry I shall bring her food."

"Gracias Beatriz, I'm starving."

I followed Fernando to the round table of five guys. Two had their backs to me, but the three I could see were good looking. All five had similar hair, jet-black, except for one. His hair was black with caramel highlights. I couldn't see his face.

"*Vale* Gentlemen," Fernando said. "Kasey, I would like you to meet the finest young men and best customers in Deia." Fernando extended his hand out as we stopped in front of the table.

As if choreographed, the men stood for formal introductions. We exchanged courteous smiles. I glanced over at the two men that I couldn't see before. They were significantly taller than I, except the twins. The caramel haired one was exquisite, aristocratic. His smile was warm, yet at the same time savagely alluring. His dark eyes were mysterious as if he could see through me. I glanced away. The last man was shaggy, unkempt; with hairy eyebrows, mustache, beard, and mid-shoulder length long hair.

"It is quite a pleasure to make your acquaintance, Kasey. I am Max Kleon." The one with a tie and suit said in a funny British accent extending his hand. I took it and shook back, speechless. He seemed older than me, with deep black eyes and a large nose. The other two sitting next to Max Kleon were twins, mirror images, except for the different color tee shirts.

"He is one of two doctors we have here in Deia and the oldest of the Kleons," Fernando offered more information. That would explain the attire.

"These are his brothers, the twins, John and Martin," Fernando said towards the two youngest of the group. Each said "Hello" and I replied the same in return.

"I am Antony, the second oldest." The one with the shaggy beard spoke up. He extended his hand and I met it with a reply of, "Nice to meet you Antony."

Finally, Fernando introduced him.

"This is Dion." Fernando put his arm around Dion's shoulders as if he were a son of his.

Dion extended his hand, keeping his smile, "Delighted to meet you, Kasey."

I took no breaths as I reached out to shake his hand. When our hands embraced, his skin felt baby soft. He shook my hand with the strength of a gentle wind. He didn't let it go immediately, he held onto it a second longer than he needed to.

"It's a pleasure," I replied in a whispered voice, dazed and awestruck.

"Humph," Max cleared his throat, "My dear, we have all been told of your stay here from America. Where 'bouts in the States are you from?"

I heard his question but couldn't put a coherent thought together. His brother, Dion's eyes left me unable to form words. I struggled for an answer. "From St. Cloud... in Florida."

Max smiled fully aware I lacked sense.

"That is near Disney, is it not?" One of the twins asked. Which twin was John or Martin?

"Yes, have you been there?"

"Not in a long time," Antony chimed in.

"I bet we will be seeing that place again soon." The other twin said as he grinned.

I found the comment odd especially when the other brothers chuckled.

"Why's that?" I asked.

"Here comes Beatriz with your food. Come Kasey, gentlemen *un gusto*," Fernando said. He started to lead me away. Forgetting my previous question I quickly said, "It was a pleasure to meet all of you."

"And the same here. I am sure we will be seeing quite a bit of you," Max answered. They all resumed their seats.

I followed Fernando to a table at the back of the restaurant near the kitchen door. Beatriz placed a plate on the table with shrimp and what looked like scallop potatoes. To accompany the food, Fernando filled a glass with red wine. Steam rose from the plate. I smelled the succulent aromas of seafood and seasonings. But a feeling of intrigue about the brothers overcame me. They each had auras filled with mystery, especially Dion. He locked me in with his eyes. I wanted to turn and take a glimpse in their direction. Were they discussing me? I sat down at my table and took a quick glance. Dion caught me looking and smiled. Embarrassed, I turned away.

"This smells wonderful. What is it?"

"I hope you do not mind zesty hot. It's spicy shrimp with garlic and olive oil cooked with *patatas* in *Alioli* sauce," Beatriz answered.

"I don't know what *patatas* are, but this is delicious!" I tried to remember my best table manners, but I wanted to scarf it down. I was starving, and the food was heavenly.

"*Patatas* are potatoes," Fernando informed me.

"Thank you so much. It's okay for me to have the red wine?" I was not used to drinking. I think I could count the number of drinks I had in my life on one hand.

"Yes, of course," Beatriz said.

"I've actually never had a glass of real wine before. I have had wine coolers."

"No real *vino*?" Fernando asked, shocked.

"No, not ever. The drinking age in the States is legally twenty-one."

"Well, here it is eighteen," Fernando said.

"I turned eighteen last month." I was aware that the drinking age in Spain was eighteen. I researched that before I came over.

"Then *perfecto*! No proper meal is enjoyed without a glass of wine." Fernando placed the glass in my hand.

I brought the glass slowly to my lips tilted it until the dark juice barely touched my lips. I sipped a small amount. It was strong and burned going down. Its flavor was potent and had an oak taste afterward. I made the face you make after you have just swallowed bad tasting medicine.

"You do not like it?" Beatriz asked.

"Keep drinking. You will get used to it," Fernando urged.

"Oh, it's just different. It is very heavy. I'm not used to it. That's all. Thank you," I took another sip and placed it down on the table.

"Kasey, what are your plans for tomorrow?" Fernando asked.

"I have to go to the school in Palma, fill out my paper work, and meet with the representative. I start my classes this Monday. Is there some way I can get to the school?"

"Hmm, we have a car, but Beatriz is taking the children into San Marina tomorrow to pick up some fresh fish for the restaurant."

"Oh, is there a bus?" I asked.

A voice from behind jolted me.

"No need to ride the bus. I will be more than glad to take her down to the school. It is on my way to the theater and truly no problem," Dion said.

My heart stopped. I must have looked terrified because he leaned his head down toward me and said, "You look concerned, I do not bite and I am a safe driver."

His light musky scent left a trail behind as he leaned back.

"Dion that would be wonderful! *Muchas gracias*. You boys are always so helpful." Fernando stood up to shake his hand.

"Yes, thank you." I half a smiled at him, then turned my eyes to my plate.

"It is my pleasure. Fernando here is our bill." He handed the check holder to Fernando and said, "I shall see you at nine, Kasey."

Then he turned to go.

## 2. Kasey's Hostile Beginnings

After the scrumptious meal, Beatriz escorted me through the kitchen door up a flight of stairs. The staircase was long and straight with a hazed glass, French door at the top. The living room's linen and sand drapes complemented the maple wood floors. Modest white furniture evenly spread out through the room. Very Feng Shui.

"And the first door on your left is the boy's room. They have own bathroom," Beatriz talked on and on about the rooms and the family schedule in the mornings. I pretended to hear every word, but my mind was on nine o'clock tomorrow morning and Dion.

"Your room is across from the boy's," Beatriz continued.

Why would he have offered to take me tomorrow? He doesn't know me! Were all Spaniards like this?

"I leave you now. If you have any question ask Catalina, she is in her room. You maybe want to rest."

"I do Beatriz, *gracias*. After that long flight I could use a nap."

"Oh, yes, *este es su casa*. This is your home, now." She turned and walked through the living room and out the front door.

I grabbed the ornate brass handle to what would be my room for the next ten months, pulled it down, and walked in. The room was the size of an extra-large walk-in closet. A twin-size bed with green and blue floral bed sheets sat under a small open window. A little wooden desk next to a large wooden armoire was parallel to the bed. A light salty breeze blew in. My suitcase sat in the middle of my tiny room, while the duffel bag and backpack were on my bed. I walked in and shut the door behind me, moved everything from the bed onto the floor and threw myself onto the bed. I took a deep breath to decompress.

Unable to relax, I sat still for a few seconds before popping up onto one side. My hand dove into the front pocket of my backpack, and pulled out my recently upgraded Blackberry. It was my parents going away present with an international calling plan. I pressed the number one, then the green send button. It rang.

"Hey *chica*! How's the other side of the world?" said a low crackling voice.

"I haven't been gone but a day and your voice sounds lower. Did your Adam's apple drop while I was gone?" I replied to my little brother.

"My voice hasn't change it's the new hemisphere that's got your ear drums messed up."

"Sure, that's it. How are things there?" I asked, a small lump in my throat starting to form. I tried to control my voice.

"Don't start. Come on suck it up. You're a tough cookie. Things don't change here. You're the one on the adventure, remember."

"Yeah, I know. What about Sue and Frankie?"

My parents never liked the words Mom and Dad. They felt people shouldn't have status names forced on them. They considered themselves earthy people. My brother and I always did whatever we wished, whether my parents agreed to it or not. Our childhood was one bizarre experience after another.

"They went to Cocoa Beach to watch a Native American drum show," Nolan answered indifferent.

"And you didn't go because…" I emphasized the 'because.'

"I don't know. They're acting really loopy right now. Like, loopier than they normally are. I think your leaving has made them flip some. Or something's up."

"Really? I didn't gather that from them when I left. They aren't like that. Are you sure?" Why were my carefree parents now, after eighteen years, giving a damn?

"I don't know, they're just weird," Nolan sounded fed up with them already.

"Nolan sweetie, we've known this since birth. That's why we stuck together in our fight for normal."

"Yeah, but now you're on the other side of the world. How do I not go crazy over here?" My leaving was getting to him.

"It's not like it can get any worse, you know what to expect from them. Make yourself scarce. Try hanging out at Tim's house. As soon as school starts, it won't be bad. You will be okay, I promise."

Would he? Could he handle independence and no structure without me there?

"Yea, I'll keep busy and try to stay out of sight for the next few weeks. It's just not the same without you around here."

The minute I turned eighteen, I ran from them, and from him. Did I abandon him?

"I know. I miss you too. But you know this is a great opportunity for me and something I had to do." The lump in my throat hardened, I tried not to cry.

"I never said I missed you. Just that it's quieter around here."

I could hear the tease in my brother's voice. I smiled.

"I'll call you soon, enough. Tell Sue and Frankie I arrived and that I'm fine. Love ya."

"Take care, Sis. Keep me up to date. Bye."

The phone clicked off. Letting out a big, sad sigh, I stood and put my duffel bag on my bed. Feeling like a mother bear deserting her cub, I worried about him. How could I have left him for so long in the care of my parents? Or lack of care. They never did much looking after us. I hoped he was strong enough to be independent and that his twelve-year-old instincts would kick in. I unzipped and opened the bag. The airport security had rummaged through my belongings leaving a mess. I took out my toiletries and wondered if I would be able to keep them in the bathroom.

I could hear low rock music coming from under the door of the bathroom. Catalina and I shared a bathroom, each having our own door. I slid open my door and saw that Catalina's was also open. Good, I thought, perhaps I could ask her. I stepped through the bathroom and peered into her room. Her room mirrored mine including matching furniture, but hers was decorated to match the bathroom, black and white. Hanging above her bed was a big poster of a rock band. I didn't recognize the group, I guessed they were European.

I knocked on the doorframe. "Hi, I was wondering if I can keep my toiletries in the bathroom or should I put them in…"

"Keep them where want," she said in a low harsh voice without ever turning around from her computer.

"Okay, thanks. Can I ask you a question?"

"Not if you value your pathetic life," she answered, still not looking up from her computer.

Shocked by her blunt rudeness I asked, "Can I ask, what's up? Have I done something?"

That got her attention. She turned around sharply, "What did you say?"

"Why are you so short with me? We don't even know each other."

She got up from her computer and stood right in front of me, "I do not like Americans!" She slammed the door shut.

I didn't expect her to be a mean bigot. I'd get the scoop on her. I went back into my room, unpacked all of my belongings, then lay down for a nap.

Groggy, I moaned as my hungry stomach woke me. I rolled over and fell off the bed with a thud.

"Ow."

A knock on my door followed by a, "*Estas bien?*" It sounded like Garcia.

I got up and opened the door, rubbing my shoulder. "Yeah, I'm okay… not used to a twin bed."

"Oh," Garcia said.

Behind him came a smaller voice, "You have slept a long time!" Rodrigo pushed past me and into the room.

"Rodrigo! *No entres*! She has not invited you in." Garcia scolded his little brother.

"It's all right. I don't mind, you guys can come in." They both did and sat on my bed. I took a seat in the wooden desk chair.

"What time is it?" I asked.

"It is nine; we finished dinner about a half hour ago. Everybody came to see you but you were asleep. You can go downstairs and grab some if you want." Garcia was very helpful.

"Everybody? What do you mean?" I asked.

"*Tio* Armando, *Tia* Carmen, Carlos, both Marias, Eduardo…" Rodrigo was going on and on with names.

"Hold on. Who are all these people, and why did they come to see me?"

"Aunts, uncles, cousins. They usually come to have dinner. They all wanted to meet you." Garcia smiled.

"I see. I come from a small family just my parents, brother, and me."

"That's it?" My new little brother was adorably cute.

# Men of the Cave

"Yup, I can't believe how late it is. You guys eat dinner late!"

"It is normal for *aqui*, oh sorry, 'here'," Rodrigo said.

"I am hungry," I said.

"What is Walt Disney World like?" Rodrigo blurted out as if he'd waited a long time to ask me this.

"It's the happiest place on Earth, truly," I smiled knowing he would relish the answer. Garcia rolled his eyes.

"Okay, you asked me a question, and now it's my turn. What's up with Catalina?"

"She is a brat," Garcia mumbled.

"She is crazy!" Rodrigo exclaimed.

"Crazy?" I questioned.

"She is not crazy!" Garcia rolled his eyes.

"She told me she didn't like Americans."

"Oh, she does not. I would sleep *con un hojo abrierto* and watch your back." Rodrigo warned.

"Rodrigo! She is not crazy like that," Garcia said, trying to shut his brother up.

"Wait did he tell me to sleep with one eye open?" I asked concerned.

"Yes, but do not listen to him. Let us go. She needs to eat." They got up and walked out the door.

"Hmm," I said. As I was about to click off the light and follow them out, the toilet flushed. Great. That meant Miss Black Nightmare was listening to our conversation.

When I passed the living room, I noticed pictures that I hadn't before. It was a wall of photographs. In the center was a big eight by ten photo of the Castillo family. Fernando and Beatriz stood behind four children sitting in a row from oldest to youngest. First, a girl who looked like Beatriz, then a pre-teen Catalina, next to her was Garcia, about eight or nine years old and last, Rodrigo as a toddler. I wondered who this other girl was. She must be an older sister, but no one had mentioned her. I found it odd. Maybe she was away. I ran downstairs to try the swordfish.

## 3. Dion's Mini Cooper

I pulled up to El Caracoles restaurant ten minutes early. I do not know why I offered to drive Kasey. Am I letting destiny take her course? I walked through the restaurant and greeted Fernando in the kitchen.

"*Buenos Dias Señor* Fernando. *Buenos Dias señores,*" I greeted all the men working in the kitchen.

"*Buenos Dias* Dion. Go ahead upstairs, Kasey's room is the first door on the right," Fernando said, not even looking up from the parsley he was chopping.

"*Gracias Señor,* have a lovely day." I passed the busy cooks and walked up the stairs.

Entering their home, I noticed it had not changed since I was there for the wake. I knocked twice on Kasey's door and heard drawers slamming. The knob on the door turned and broke my contemplation.

She opened the door and with a brilliant smile and said, "*Buenos Dias,* come in."

Waiting what seemed like centuries for this moment, I returned her smile. I reached my hand delicately, under her ear.

She flinched. Her eyes danced. I pressed my lips onto her cheek and said smoothly, *"Buenos Dias."* I let go of her and walked into the room.

"Yeah, that's something that's going to take some getting used to." She flushed. Her cheeks now red contrasted against her pale skin. Her hair dazzled me, so red, so vibrant. It was like a light wavy scarlet scarf that accented the natural green jewels that were her eyes. In seconds, I knew her facial features. Then I studied the rest of her.

"You're early," she said.

"Actually on time. Would you like for me to wait downstairs and give you more time?"

The red and black colors of her paisley tank stood out against her pale skin. The shirt stopped above the crescent rim of her breasts, and I could only see a handful of brownish freckles above the shirt line. Her frame was smallish, somewhat petite. I think she caught me observing her because she narrowed her eyes in a disapproving manner. I shifted my gaze to her face.

"No, that's fine. I'll be ready in a sec. I have to pack my bag." She reached for a small black bag and placed it on the desk. She began stocking it with pens, pencils, and notebooks. Catalina stood at the doorway, peering in. She wore her typical Goth inspired attire.

*"Buenos Dias,* Dion," she said.

*"Hola* Catalina, how are you this fine morning?"

"Okie-Dokie," she replied, sarcastic.

"I thought you were going to San Marina with your mother today," Kasey said.

I could feel the tension between the two young women.

"My ride is downstairs." Catalina ignored Kasey then stormed off. Kasey faced me clearly bothered by the interaction.

"Ready?" she asked.

"Always." I reached out and grabbed her bag with a smile. She returned my grin, which I took as a thank you. As we walked out of the restaurant, she made a face.

"Don't tell me your car is the Mini Coop convertible?"

"Ah, but of course madam. Allow me to give you the ride of your life in this exquisite vehicle." I impersonated a chauffeur.

"Oh, okay, sure." She sat on the white leather. I cleaned the car the night before making sure that all the trash was out and it smelled nice.

"So why this car?" she asked as I started the auto and began to drive.

"An automobile is not some piece of machine you merely pick. It is an accessory to a personality." I felt like educating her on my theories between man and machine.

"Really," she said. "Then you know what my next question will be."

"I chose the Mini Coop convertible because it has a gentle way. It grooves and moves with the winding roads of Mallorca. It can have unexpected speed and strength. The black and white colors, well, that is simply because there is nothing better than the classic tuxedo look."

"Wow, Dion. How James Bond of you."

"James Bond?" I did not particularly like the comparison she made. "I hope to think that I am not nearly as self-absorbed as James Bond."

"I suppose that's to be seen," she said with a hint of intrigue.

"Well then, what car did you drive in the states?" I asked.

"An old Saturn."

I winced at her. "It does not sound like you had a good relationship."

"I guess not, it got me where I needed to go," Kasey said.

"Was it at least fire red or emerald green like your features?" I asked.

"No, it was grey," she said with a slight grin.

"Then my theory is obviously flawed."

"Did you spill a bottle of perfume in here?" She rubbed her nose.

"The store called it warm meadow. I sprayed it on the floor mats."

"Oh, it's potent." Her face showed disapproval.

"So Kasey," I changed the subject. "Is that your true name?"

"No, it's Kassandra."

"Why do you go by Kasey?"

"My parents have always called me that. It just stuck."

"I like Kassandra. I think it be fits you better. Does it bother you if people call you that?"

"We hardly know each other and already you're changing my name," she teased.

"I was simply asking a question. I would never do anything without your consent."

I could already sense the strong chemistry between us. We were natural with each other. I could not help myself but to be flirtatious with her. I would have to tread this liaison with great care.

"Call me what you like. I don't mind either way."

As we drove up the winding roads away from the village, off to the side, Catalina walked into a forest path.

"I wonder where she's going," Kasey said, glancing backwards.

"There are ancient ruins about one mile into the forest."

Kasey whipped her head around.

"What does she do there?"

"She conducts meditation rituals to contact her dead sister."

"What!" Kasey's eyes went wide. Clearly, she did not expect this answer.

"Four years ago Elena Castillo died in a car accident. Catalina's never let her go." I retold Kasey the key facts of the past while my mind flashed back to the night of the accident.

\*\*\*\*\*\*

The evening was hot and dry; the kind of dry that made it hard to breathe. The little champagne sedan was destroyed on all sides from the impact of rolling down the rocks and then smashing onto the ground below. My brothers and I reached the site seconds after the car drove off the cliff. We were too late. It was busy and hectic in all the chaos. I helped Max with Elena while Antony, John, and Martin went to help the American boy Elena was dating. The impact instantly killed him. Thrown from the car, his body landed on the ground in front of it. He died with his face forever screaming in fear. Elena was smashed almost flat between the steering wheel and her seat. I pried her out and let Max get to work. She was barely alive and dying right before us. The damage to her body was so severe that it was beyond repair. Max could only keep her comfortable until she died. Antony made the sign of the cross on both their foreheads and recited the rite of passage. When Antony finished, we prayed for their souls. I placed her back into the car as best I could so that everything was just as it was. Then we departed the scene.

******

"The American tourist Elena was dating drove the car off a cliff," I said, looking straight ahead.

"Why?" Kasey whispered.

"The authorities say they do not know."

"But you do! I mean you sound like you know more," she said with suspicion.

I looked over at her with a serious face. "I know only what the authorities know." I hoped she picked up my hint. I did not wish to discuss the matter further.

"But I mean someone doesn't do something like that without a reason. How long were they dating? What did Fernando and Beatriz think of the relationship? Was he normal or did he have some screws loose? Did..."

"Kasey, I really do not care to discuss this matter." I interrupted her and kept my eyes on the road.

She faced her window and huffed, "Fine."

The few minutes left of the ride were done in silence. I pulled into the tiny parking lot of the school. In the smoothest voice I could muster I said, "I shall be here around one to escort you back home."

She opened the door to the Mini Coop and mumbled coldly, "Fine."

I reached out and gently grabbed her wrist to stop her from leaving the car. She gave me a cross look as if I had overstepped a boundary.

"My apologies," I said removing my hand. "May I see your phone?"

"My phone?"

"Please." I extended my hand out and attempted a charming look. She reached into her bag and placed the phone in my hand.

I quickly punched in my phone number using only my thumb. "Now, you have my number."

She nodded and stepped out. Her mood had turned cold and sorrowful over Elena's tragedy. Perhaps the ride back would be lighter. I stared at her perfect thin curves through my rearview mirror. Her white Capri pants hung just below her hipbone while the paisley halter-top sat above the hipbones leaving a perfect inch of skin exposed. Her arms carried the weight of many beaded bracelets. A light breeze blew a few curly strands of hair down. Her half up-do would surely fall from its clip by the day's end with Mallorca's wind gusts. What was I thinking falling for this beautiful gypsy?

I stared blankly into the same road I drove for the past four years, but my mind was on anything but the ride. She was the perfect imperfection for me. How could God have created such a soul for me? More to the question, why would He have? My phone vibrated and not a second later the overture of the Phantom of the Opera played from my mobile. The screen lit up, Twin One.

"Hello, John," I answered.

"Hello, my brother. Martin and I were here bugging around and wanted to know what you thought of Kasey. Were we right?"

I sighed, "Yes, you chaps were dead on."

"Martin says she left mad. What could you possibly have said?"

"Quit using your abilities on us," I growled into the phone. I was never fond of their gift to see into the future. Laughter exploded from the other end.

"Yeah, yeah, we will not look into her future anymore. We promise. Thing is, you do not have the most experience with the ladies. You could use our help."

"What? Little boys, that is rubbish."

The chuckling continued.

"Look, I am almost to practice. We shall speak later." I cut them off.

"Later then. May I offer some advice? Keep the conversation light on the way back, pick up some lunch, and go to church," John said.

"Church?" I questioned.

"Yes, for I am sure there was nothing good going on in that head of yours. At least, not from what I saw your eyes doing through the rearview mirror."

"When I get home I am going to get you…," I screamed into the cell. He hung up. I drove into the parking lot of the open-air Greek style amphitheater. The stone staircase sloped down toward the stage. Located in the valley of the mountain, the view was serene, heavenly. Zen and peace captured into this magnificent facility.

******

It was one thirty and Kasey had not come out to the school's parking lot. I was about to go in search of her when she exited with a friend.

"Dion, I'm sorry I hope you haven't been waiting long," Kasey said with a smile. She was clearly over her hollow mood from earlier.

"To wait is simply life in slow motion."

I went to 'greet' her the Spanish way. This time she expected it and returned the greeting onto both my cheeks.

"This is Madhu, she's staying in Vallendosa."

Madhu was clearly not Spanish, based on her dark brown skin and her name. I placed her origins somewhere in India.

"*Mucho gusto,*" I greeted her. "How long have you been here?"

"I have been here since the start of summer from Bangladesh," she said in a British accent. She was quite attractive, but very flamboyant in her orange and green attire and tight skirt. I liked and appreciated Kasey's subtle simplicity.

"So, are you sweet?" I asked Madhu with a grin. She smiled and Kasey looked at me as if I were insane.

"Oh, absolutely," Madhu said with a huge smirk. "Kasey, my name means honey. Apparently Dion knows this."

"I am fluent in various languages." I chimed in to help poor Kasey understand.

"That should come in handy some times," she said, rather impressed. Or so I hoped she was impressed.

"Kasey, I have to get going. I shall give you a call tomorrow and we can coordinate your sightseeing tour, Madhu style."

"Ok, I'm looking forward to it. *Gracias, adios,*" Kasey gave Madhu a hug.

"Dion, *un gusto,*" Madhu nodded toward me.

"Also a pleasure for me as well," I replied. She walked back into the building. I looked at Kasey, relieved to be in her company again. As I predicted, her hair had completely fallen loose. She was wearing it down and wild.

"Did you have a good day?" I opened the car door for her.

"I did! It is going to be hard to pick up the language as well as they expect. These two semesters are going to be great."

'Great', I thought. I hoped this year, for her at least, would be life altering, and more than just 'great.' I got in and started the car. As we drove the winding roads again, I glanced over at her. I was having a hard time keeping my eyes off her. I could feel myself analyzing her every detail. Then to make matters worse, she turned her head and caught me staring. She gave me a slight grin. I didn't look away. I returned the grin and continued to gaze between her and the road.

"Thank you for the ride today." She interrupted my thoughts.

"You are very welcome. It has been enjoyable. If you would like, I can drive you around anytime you need," I extended the offer knowing she would accept it later.

"Thank you. I've got your number if I need it…"

"You will." I broke in with a smile.

She huffed and turned to look out the window.

"So," she said. "How was the movie?"

"Movie?" I asked.

She looked at me perplexed. "Didn't you say that you were going to the theater?"

I gave a laugh, "No I did not go to that type of theater." I clearly confused her further.

"I don't understand," she said.

"I went to the stage theater."

"Oh," she realized. "Did you go see a play?"

"No, I went to practice for one."

"Practice? So you are in a play?" She inquired.

"Yes. I am an actor at the local theater."

"Really!" Apparently, this was a good thing. I should definitely elaborate.

"Yes, we are putting on the play of Hercules in three months."

"Hercules, that's exciting. What's your part?"

"I am Hercules."

"No, you're not! You have the lead!"

Did she doubt my acting abilities? I would have to show her.

"Yes, I am a good actor."

She giggled.

"What do you find amusing?"

"Definitely a bit of James Bond in you," she answered.

"Agh," I scoffed.

Once in Deia I parallel parked in front of an alleyway.

"Where are we? What are we doing?" Kasey sounded alarmed.

"Relax, I am treating you to lunch and picking up some for my brothers as well. Did I not mention this?"

"Lunch! I thought you always asked permission?" She got out of the car and put her hands on her hips.

I smiled, "So one slipped."

"Where are we? These look like residential homes?" She asked gazing around. The street was deserted. I reached out and grabbed her hand.

"Follow me it is down the alley," I pulled her arm heading toward the shadowy alley. She halted and took her hand out of mine.

"Where are we going, Dion? This part of town looks really old, and there aren't any restaurants here." She questioned with an alarmed tone to her voice. Her body turned tense and tight.

"Forgive me Kasey. Please do not be troubled. I have someone I think you would like to meet. She lives in the last door down the alley." I extended my hand out to her, "Please."

Her eyes narrowed the way they so often do. She glanced down the alley and then looked into my eyes. She searched for something that would let her know to trust me. Whatever it was she saw, she loosened her body, and walked past my hand into the alley.

## 4. Kasey and the Villagers

I could feel my heart thump against my skin. I would never have done this back home, but the American in Spain said try something out of your comfort zone. I was scared, nervous, but every time I looked at him my intuition screamed trust him.

There wasn't a soul in the alley. On either side of the barely lit passage, were five green doors. One was by itself at the end of the alleyway. We kept going deeper and deeper into the shadows until we stopped at the last green door.

"Dion, what are we doing here?" I whispered even though no one was around.

"Relax." He knocked on the door. Shuffling and rustling noises came from the other side. Then the door opened.

A tiny old woman with white hair done up in a bun opened the door. "*Si*," she said with a weak and creaky voice. I relaxed.

Dion answered her in a language other than Spanish. I imagined it was Catalan, the original language of the land. Dion hugged and kissed her affectionately. With a half bow, he introduced me. I gathered that much from the conversation. She leaned forward, expecting me to greet her. I did as Dion had.

The apartment was like a medieval furnished chamber. It was dreary inside. Only two dimmed orange lamps. One of the lamps sat in the sitting area, while the other in the dining. Had I time warped into the dark ages? How could such a murky place exist in the beautiful paradise of Deia?

Dion and the elderly woman kept talking in the odd dialect. Then she left the room through a paint chipped red door.

"Dion, who is she?" I continued to whisper, "Are you speaking Catalan?"

He spoke in a normal tone. "No, Greek. Her name is Helena. She is a dear old friend. She is blind."

"She gets around quick and without any help." I was impressed.

"This place has not changed in a hundred years. I did not bring you here simply because she is a great cook. Helena has been in Deia for as long as I can remember."

"Really?"

"She is like a grandmother to me. That is why I brought you to meet her. She is an impressive story teller." He gestured for me to sit on the medieval couch.

Instead of cushions, her sofas had brick colored leather that wrapped around dark squared pieces of wood. It attached at the seams with large bronze metal buttons. They were flat and looked hard. The leather had intricate etched drawings of a matador spearing his bull. The furniture barely fit in the tiny apartment.

Her couches were as hard and tough as they looked. He sat next to me, our knees touched. I cherished every breath of his strong masculine cologne. He was tender here in this apartment. I sensed this was a place of home to him. He was gorgeous. Every feature on his face perfect, dark and inviting. The boy could be his own photo shoot.

"Story teller?"

"She tells stories of ancient Greece. If you like history, she can really enlighten you."

"Greek mythology is boring. I didn't care for it in school." I struggled with the subject, it was just one long made up soap opera.

He laughed, "Do not tell her that. She has a lot of pride with those old stories. She is truly an extraordinary woman and a great cook."

"You've mentioned that twice. What makes her food so great?"

"Her food is traditional. It makes me feel like I am in another time." He smiled as if remembering the past. I thought it was an unusual comment to make about food, but before I could inquire, Helena came out and interrupted my thoughts. Dion said she was blind, but she entered the room carrying three plates and silverware and placed them appropriately on the table. I could tell that her glazed grey eyes only stared straight. She said something to Dion then returned into the kitchen.

"What did she say?" I asked.

"She said the food will be out soon, and then she will meet you."

"Meet me?"

"She will probably touch your face to see what you look like."

"Oh." I understood. I'd never known anyone who was blind. "Does she have any family here?" I felt sorry for the lonely old woman.

"No, but the people of this village love her. She gets many visitors daily. She makes my brothers and I lunch four times a week."

"Wait, she makes you lunch? Fernando told me that you have dinner at his restaurant almost every day! Do you boys ever cook or eat at home? What about your parents? Do they eat out too?"

"No, my brothers and I are horrible in the kitchen, so we will not cook."

"Agh, typical," I disapproved.

He smirked.

"My parents died a long time ago. Max has taken care of us ever since," he said with no emotion.

"Oh, I'm so sorry." I wished I'd known this information or I would have never brought it up.

"It is quite all right. We have adjusted."

Helena came out with a pot and set it on the table. She walked over to us. Dion stood, and I followed his lead. He said something to her and then said my name. She smiled and leaned in as if to give me a hug. I stepped forward so she could find me. She reached out and placed both her hands on the creases of my cheekbones. Then she brushed my cheek with a ghostlike kiss. I went to step back, but she didn't let go. She held my face with both hands and lightly stroked all my facial features with her fingertips. She said a few things to Dion, and he would reply. When she was satisfied, she stepped back and smiled. She said something then headed for the dining room table.

He chuckled and blushed.

"What did she say?" I whispered to Dion.

"She said red heads have tempers," he said with a laugh.

"She did not! Did she?"

"Most certainly, she did." Dion lead me to my seat.

"Wait, how can she tell what color my hair is?"

He looked away laughing.

"Dion! You're such a liar what did she really say?"

"She said you were unique." He sat across from me.

"Unique, in what way?"

"She said you reminded her of Pandora."

"Pandora! As in, the Greek myth of the first woman Zeus created and let all the evil in the world out from her box?"

"Actually it was a jar. That is her." He held his bowl out as Helena filled it with the porridge.

"That's weird. As if she knows what she looks like?" I held out my bowl and Helena kept pouring. She somehow knew when the bowl was full. It didn't really smell like anything at all, but the steam rose from the three bowls.

"Mmmm, enjoy! I simply love her porridge." Dion lifted a big spoon, blew on it, and stuck it right into his mouth.

I raised my spoon and blew on it. I dipped the tip of my tongue into the spoon to verify its temperature. It was surprisingly much cooler than I'd originally thought. I stuck the whole spoon in my mouth, expecting a vibrant explosion of flavors. I got nothing. The porridge tasted like bland vegetables and boiled meat. It had no salt, no seasoning, and no spice at all.

I glanced over to Dion who was eating it right up and enjoying every bite. Were my taste buds crazy? I tried another spoonful, nothing, no flavor. I ate my porridge like a good houseguest. I was in complete awe at how much Dion enjoyed this meal.

Helena packed a pot full for him to take to his brothers. She told captivating stories of ancient Greek heroes with intricate details. She was extremely talented at embellishing the imagination to bring realism to those mythical tales. After a few hours, we said our farewells and left her to her dark home.

"Thank you for bringing me here. Her stories were amazing. I'm keeping a travel log of my trip. I'll have to write this down tonight so that I can remember every detail," I said to Dion as he opened the door to the Mini Cooper for me.

"It was my pleasure, Kasey." He gave me his usual charming smile. I blushed and looked away.

The ride back to the restaurant was too short. I wanted to spend more minutes, hours, every second with Dion. I delayed my leaving his car before I said, "Thank you for today. I had fun."

"It was absolutely memorable."

"Okay," I said.

I reach for the door handle, but he held my arm.

"Please, wait, allow me." He opened his car door, stepped out, and walked around to my door and opened it for me. I took the hand he offered and let him help me out.

"A lady should never leave an automobile without at least being offered proper assistance. I would have offered the other times, but you were so quick to leave my car you did not give me a chance." He closed the door behind me.

"Ohhhh, I'm so not in the States anymore."

He gave me a curious gaze. "A proper gentlemen needs to let any lady riding in his vehicle know that he will care for her."

There was something unexplainable about this guy, something attractive. "You act so prehistoric. It's odd."

He laughed.

"I am not that old," he mumbled. "I'll see you Sunday morning."

"Sunday?"

"Catholicism is strong within this village. Everyone attends mass on Sunday."

"Ah." I nodded. It had not dawned on me that I would have to participate in the religious ceremonies of my host family. I didn't know how to feel. I'd never set foot in a church, nor did I buy into the philosophies they tried to sell.

He kissed my cheek then got in his car and drove off.

******

Deia on Sundays resembled a ghost town. All six hundred and fifty inhabitants made it to the Catholic Church that day. The Castillo's insisted that I attend the service with them. We went to an early mass around seven thirty in the morning. I took my journal to make observations of their customs. I wasn't really going to take part of the rituals of their faith. Beatriz and Catalina covered their hair with a small black veil. Beatriz offered me a headdress. I did not want to offend her, so I respectfully placed it on my head.

The sandstone church sat on top of a hill, off to it's distance the mountain and the rocky shoreline. The Mass was full of chants, I had a hard time following. The Kleon brothers were heavily involved as readers and altar servers. It was hard to focus on what was occurring. I was too busy watching Dion.

The villagers stared or snarled at me because I wasn't praying and bowing my head when required. I sat next to Beatriz and wrote down notes in my journal. The town was strict in their religious beliefs. Catholicism is huge in Spain. The mass unnerved me. If required by the Castillos, I would attend, but I hoped they would let me stay home.

After the service, the Castillos socialized with friends. This Sunday they had many friends wanting to get the scoop on me. They were cordial and fascinated by my foreign self. Among their friends were the Kleon brothers. They greeted me as they would a member of the Castillo family.

"You look lovely," Dion said as he kissed my cheek. He gazed at my green skirt and black halter-top.

"Thanks, I don't think your opinion was shared by the locals." I had gotten nasty looks from some of the elderly women.

"They are not used to uncovered shoulders at church."

"I wish someone would have told me," I shrugged.

"It is all right to come as you are comfortable. Did you enjoy the service?" He was extremely polite. It was hard to converse with him while he wore his altar server robes. He resembled a priest, and I felt he shouldn't be fraternizing with me.

"Not really," I answered.

Concerned he said, "I am sorry to hear that." He seemed confused as if he didn't understand something.

"Is everything all right?"

"Fate has perplexed me." He shook his head as if shaking his thoughts away. Before I could inquire further, Beatriz interrupted us.

"Kasey, we are leaving now. Dion have a blessed day," she said in her angelic voice.

"*Señora*, you as well." He gave her a kiss on her cheek. I turned to follow Beatriz, but Dion took my hand. I stopped, allowing him to hold it.

He swallowed, "You enjoy your afternoon as well my dear." He leaned forward and gently placed his lips to my forehead. I held my breath. He let go of my hand and took a step back.

"Thank you," I scarcely got out the words. I looked away and started toward Beatriz and Fernando. I trembled. What was I doing? I didn't come to Spain to have a fling. Quite the opposite. The last thing I wanted was another emotional rollercoaster. Poor Dion, he was definitely interested. I would be lying to myself if I said I was anything less as well.

## 5. Kasey's Family

"*Hola, caballeros.* What will it be today?" I said with my American accent to Dion and his brothers.

"Good evening Kasey. How has this fine Friday treated you?" Max asked in his proper way with his proper attire.

"Very well, thank you," I blushed. He had such a way with words.

"I would like my usual vegetarian meal, please." Antony roughly put his menu away. He was the strange one, always rather grubby, or un-groomed would be the better term.

"How have you liked your first two months in Spain, Kasey? Are you enjoying yourself?" Max ignored Antony and looked at me.

"Oh, of course. It's a different world over here compared to the states. I wish I had passed the international driving test, so I can drive myself around."

"I am quite sure Dion does not mind taking you to school every morning," John snickered.

I noticed some kind of communication pass between the brother's eyes. Dion looked exquisite. He wore a sleek royal blue linen shirt with tan pants. His dark features made the perfect contrast against the vibrant blue of his shirt. He had slick but messy hair. He always appeared as if he was going out to a club. That style worked for him. It looked sexy.

"It is a pleasure for me to assist someone who needs my help," Dion said giving John a look that read 'cut it out.' "To start with, can I have the *Gazpacho con huevo y jamon*, please?" Dion changed the conversation.

"I would like that as well," Max said.

"That's the tomato soup with ham and eggs, right?" I asked to make sure.

"Yes," they all answered.

"John and I will have the *Aguacate con gamba* that is the avocado and prawns," Martin said.

"Thanks," I turned and headed back into the kitchen.

"*Señor* Fernando, the Kleon Brothers are here. These are the *tapas* they want." I handed him the order paper.

"Thank you, Kasey, you are a great help." He began working on the food preparation. The Castillo family had been very hospitable to me these past months. With the exception of Catalina, the rest of the family made me feel like I was one of them. They only made me work one night a week at the restaurant. The rest of the time they told me to enjoy my stay in Spain and to get my school completed. They were truly good, wholesome people.

"Are you sure you do not want something to eat for yourself?" *Señor* Fernando asked.

"I'm sure. I can't seem to get used to the ten o'clock dinners here," I said.

"Well, you ate early. When you get hungry again let me know," he said with genuine kindness.

"I'll go out and see what they want for dinner," I left the kitchen to face the Kleon brothers again.

Catalina stood at the Kleon's table taking their dinner order. I knew she was probably doing it to get a rise out of me. She was constantly doing childish annoyances to get me mad. Like the day she placed conditioner in my shampoo and shampoo in my conditioner. She denied everything, and because I think her parents are afraid of what she might do; they ignore her immaturity. She acts as if I'm a ghost. Ignores me when I speak to her and mutters comments about me when I'm right there.

I walked over to their table and said, "Thanks Catalina. You're such a great help." I gave her a fake smile.

She looked cross at me and said, "The order is done. Take it to the kitchen." She walked out of the restaurant.

"That poor child is so damaged," Max said, shaking his head sympathetic.

I let out a low giggle.

"After all the things she has done to you Kasey, you are still nice to her. I am impressed," Martin said.

"That's weird how do you know about all the things she has done?" I never told Dion about Catalina's behavior. Martin seemed nervous and the others looked at him waiting for his answer.

"I, um, heard it from Garcia." His words stumbled out.

"Well anyways, I have some strong beliefs in Karma. She has issues she needs to work out and is taking them out on me."

Dion cringed and Max shook his head as if I said something inappropriate. John and Martin smirked.

"Did I say something wrong?" I asked afraid that I'd somehow put my foot in my mouth.

"No, Kasey you are fine." Dion glanced at Max.

"Okay, I'll go put your order in."

The rest of the night was quiet. The Kleon brothers didn't say much to me again. When my shift was over, I went upstairs and sprawled across my tiny bed. It felt nice to lay back and relax. I took a few seconds to gather myself and then reached up onto the desk to grab my cell phone. I had an awful habit of checking it constantly even though I never received any messages. This time when I looked at the tiny screen, I blinked several times. The little pop up box read the number eight with Nolan's name next to it. There were no messages. My heart sunk to the bottom of my stomach. Something was wrong. Why would he call eight times and not leave a message? Frantic, I hit the call back button and held my breath with each ring. Finally, after the fifth ring, I heard his voice.

"Kasey, why haven't you called me back?" He sounded hysterical.

"I was working, what's wrong? Is everyone okay?"

"No! Kase I don't know what to do. I…I… can't take this anymore. They are nuts, completely out of their minds!" He began to bawl over the phone.

I let out a sigh of relief no one was hurt. Then I switched my tone to the understanding older sister. "Just tell me what's happened."

In between sobs he managed to say, "They...they...have joined a nudist colony. They actually think I'm going to go live with them completely naked. How can our parents be so insane?"

My mouth dropped, "What!"

"Nudist, Kasey, they have become nudist," he said calmer.

I was prepared for anything imaginable, but this.

"Oh, my God, Nolan, I don't know what to say. You're going to have to give me a minute."

"I know, I know. I thought they couldn't get any fruitier than they were. Then they go off and do this crazy thing," he said frustrated.

"Have you guys already moved into the colony?"

"No, they are doing it the first of November. When the rent goes up here; they move to the colony."

"What about the health food store?" I asked.

"They're keeping it. They're dressing for work every day, but when they are home they're going to be naked and they are going to live next to people who are naked."

"Have they said why the sudden change in life style?" I asked still in disbelief.

"They said they have always felt they wanted to live like that and since you left they thought this was the perfect opportunity. Like they don't even give a crap about me."

"Are they making you live with them?" Knowing Sue and Frankie, they would never make him do something he didn't want to.

"No, they said that if I can arrange another living situation they would let me do what I wanted, but I can have a room in their new apartment."

"Wait, what about my room?" I couldn't help but selfishly ask. Would I have a home to return to when this excursion was over?

"They said you were eighteen and more than capable living on your own. They're going to help you get a place."

"Okay, that's good." I like the thought of having my own place. "You can stay with me. I'll take care of you."

"I know you will Sis."

"So now, you have three weeks to figure out something before they move. Do you have a game plan?"

"Yeah… I do," he said hesitantly.

"Really? That's great." I felt bad for my brother. I really wished I'd been there to help him with our bizarre parents. "What are you going to do?"

"When you didn't pick up I…well, I… called him Kase. He said I could live with him, and I think I'm going to take it," he said in a whisper.

"HIM! Him who, Nolan?"

"You know who, Kase," he said gently.

"Aww, Nolan. Not Teal!"

"Kasey, I don't care what happened between you two. He was always nice to us, and we all got along with him. I'm like his brother and he'd gladly take me in. I would rather live with him over our parents. It's not going to matter for you; you are half across the world!" I heard the resentment in his voice.

"Don't you think you could've come up with another option?"

"No! You left me here with these crazy people. I have to figure out how to take care of myself because of you, and that's what I'm doing."

The tears rolled off my face. As much as I hated what was going on back home, I knew my brother would be safe and taken care of at Teal's place.

"I'm so sorry I'm not there."

"He still loves you Kase. You are all he talks about. He says you won't call him…"

"Nolan, that's none of your business."

"You can't ignore him. You were the one who was wrong."

A big lump formed in my throat, "Enough! You're going to be fine, right?"

"I guess," he mumbled.

"I love you, please take care… call me often." The tears streaked down my cheeks.

"I love you Sis, you take care too."

We hung up. I tried to call my parents. I was going to give them an earful on their ludicrous infatuation. As usual, the phone went straight to voice mail. I didn't bother wasting any more time leaving them a message. I hung up. Burrowing my face into my pillow, I wept for my little brother and my inability to help him.

## 6. Kasey and the Gladiators

Every hour of the night passed slow, unbearable. The mad behaviors of my family were a source of constant agony in my mind. In the dark hours, I felt sick to my stomach. I turned and tossed. I watched the hours go by until six o'clock in the morning. Finally, I dozed off into a deep sleep.

******

I'm standing on a cloud, a hazy mist, cool in temperature, surrounding my feet. Somehow, I move forward even though I wasn't walking. It was on a moving sidewalk. On my left, I pass a young couple sitting on a bench drinking coffee in the nude. They don't see me. I shudder with a cold chill. On my right, I pass Dion in his stunning blue shirt. He hops onto the moving sidewalk and wraps his arms around my waist. His embrace feels tight and cozy. Just ahead, I see the back of a red sofa with two people on it. In front of the couch there's a coffee table with a bonsai on it.

We approach the sofa. It spins around and another couple sits there pruning the bonsai tree. They are my parents, naked.

# Men of the Cave

"Sue! Frankie! What are you doing?" I scream. As I utter the words, Dion pushes me away with disgust. He shoves me so hard that I fall off the sidewalk and into the cool hazy mist. I fall into nowhere and nothing. Then gravity and wind start to pull my clothes off my pale body. First, I lost my shoes, and then my pants and my shirt followed. I fell into a white cool haze in only my underwear and bra. The mist is cold and my skin feels like a corpse. The haze subsides and everything is black.

That's when the strange force of nature rips off the only two garments left on me. Still falling, below me, I see I'm heading for a big black jar. The jar had hieroglyphic writings and trimmings in gold. On the top was the word *"Pandora."* I fell into the jar and the lid closed.

******

I hit the floor of my bedroom with a harsh thud. I checked myself over and was extremely relieved to see my plaid pajama pants and purple t-shirt still on my body. Taking a deep breath and pulling myself together, I glanced at the clock on the desk. If I hadn't fallen out of bed already, I would have again. It was almost eleven thirty in the morning! Thankful it was Saturday, I stretched and prepared for a run. I couldn't believe that I slept that long. I needed to decompress. Slipping into my green track shorts and pulling my hair back, I prepared my IPod. With music blaring, I concentrated on the goal to get outside and run ignoring everyone I passed in the restaurant.

I headed up the street toward the cliffs. The run was peaceful with hardly any cars on the cobblestone street.

Stunning hedges and ornate iron gates lined the road at every driveway entrance. I enjoyed pumping the salty air through my lungs. It was almost impossible to keep my mind off all the mayhem that was happening.

One thought though, one thought was a piercing knife in my mind, him. Nolan would be living with him. What was his motive for taking my brother in? Did he think I would come running into his arms when I came back? I had been avoiding his phone calls, but now I thought I owed him a chat. I wanted to talk to him about Nolan, and a small, a very small, part of me wanted to hear his voice.

After crossing the street, I came up to an open black iron gate with golden tipped spearheads. The nameplate on the gate read, "KLEON." I slowed my pace way down. All this time riding in Dion's Mini Cooper we never talked about where he lived. I was not surprised to see that the Kleons lived in an art deco style mansion. From the look of the property size, it appeared as if they owned a good chunk of land along with the beautiful home. A forest of Junipers surrounded the house. No one would ever know that the ocean lay on the other side of the mansion. I decided that a chat with Dion would be a great distraction, so I invited myself into the open gate.

Half way up the long driveway, I heard the most unusual sound. "Clink, tink, tank." The sound repeated with different rhythms. I couldn't make out what it was, but it sounded metallic. Following the sound, I walked into the forest. I didn't keep track of where I was, and realized I couldn't see the driveway or the beautiful house. I started to panic. I hoped the sounds would lead me to one of the Kleons. I trusted they could rescue my lost self. I walked toward the sound of metal clanging. It got louder as I approached.

Hidden behind tall trees, I came to a small natural clearing of low grass. In this patch, the twins battled with swords. I could tell they had been at this for a while. Sweat soaked their shaggy hair. Droplets poured down their bare muscular chests. It was hard to distinguish who was who. One wore black shorts and the other blue. They grunted with every swing, and I could see all their teenage boy muscles flex when their swords struck.

"Clink, clank," the swords sounded with each smack. Their footwork was impressive as they anticipated the other's move. They were in a dangerous synchronized dance. I recognized the swords from research for an extensive history report. The assignment was on the Roman Coliseum and the Gladiators. The men used these swords during the mid-first century. I couldn't believe the twins were fighting with this type of sword.

The swords were about two feet long with a diamond cut, pointed tip. They swung them around with ease and precision as if they were mere batons. Is this what these boys did for fun? One twin thrust his sword straight down toward the other, but he masterfully blocked the strike. I found it odd they fought with no shields like true Roman Gladiator would have. The twins locked with swords crossed, and the twin in blue fell to one knee. The twin in black, almost sinister said, "I have you now."

He swung his sword over his head like a helicopter, then aimed it dead on at his brother's chest. The twin on the floor tried to block the oncoming sword. A tragic miss. His brother's sword plunged into his chest.

I gasped as the twin fell struggling with his last few breaths. Like a movie scene, the victor's sword pierced through the young boy's body. The twin fell to the ground. The sword handle stuck out of his chest and the tip out of his back.

His brother smiled and said, "Finally," then left through a path on the other side of the clearing.

I bent over and tried to breathe. My body shook. I felt as if someone twisted my stomach like a soaked towel. I took a few steps forward and looked around. I heard nothing, only silence. I hurried to reach the brother lying dead before me.

"Martin, John…," I whispered. The boy didn't move. I took another step forward to see his face. As I peered over his shoulder, his haunting open eyes and mouth sent me into a complete earthquake. Panicked, I staggered backwards. My back felt the prickly sting of a Juniper tree. Then I ran. I sobbed, and sprinted as fast as I could. I anticipated seeing the winding driveway that would lead me out of this monstrous nightmare.

Soon, I was running on gravel, out through the open gate, and back down the road toward the restaurant. My mind was a soup of images and thoughts. Whom do I tell? I must call the police. A gladiator fight to the death! Will anyone believe me? Was all this real?

With the images in my head, I didn't realize how fast I ran back. I reached the restaurant and collapsed at the first empty table. There were no customers, Garcia placed glass cups upside down on the tables. Fernando filled vases with fresh wild flowers. Both looked at me, and based on their facial expression, I must have looked as bad as I felt. My body shook. I could barely stand. Fernando and Garcia came rushing to me.

"Kasey, *que paso!*" Fernando said with alarm. He placed his arm around my shoulders holding me up.

"Papa, *que hago?*" Garcia asked.

"Go get her some water. Tell your *Madre* in the kitchen, quickly."

Garcia ran toward the kitchen. The world started to spin.

"Kasey, what is wrong?" Fernando said urgently. The kitchen door swung open and in a matter of seconds, Garcia and Beatriz stood next to me. Garcia placed a glass in my hands. I tried to lift it but had limited control of my gross motor skills.

"Kasey…do you need to lie down?" Beatriz said, stroking back a few strands of hair.

"Papa, here comes Doctor Kleon." Garcia looked out toward the street. The world stopped spinning when I heard that. I looked up to see Max, Dion, Antony, John, and Martin sauntering toward the restaurant.

I dropped the glass. Tiny pieces of crystal splatter across the floor at my feet. I watched the Kleon brothers as if they were in slow motion walking up to us. John and Martin were, breathing, walking, and alive. Their faces looked stone serious and concerned. This couldn't be. Was I crazy? What the hell was going on? Was I even breathing? I took a quick look at the other brothers and they all had the same quizzical expression.

"Ah, Doctor Kleon. Please come. Kasey is not feeling well," Fernando said as they approached.

Max Kleon knelt down beside me, "Kasey, take slow steady breaths." He grabbed my wrist to take my pulse. "You are ice cold. Please, calm yourself," he said.

The way he said it and the way all the Kleons looked at me, they knew. They knew what I had seen. I couldn't be here. I pulled my hand away, forced myself up and ran out. I had to get away from them. They were mad! Or was it me? My ribs protested, and my legs barely worked. I headed down the sidewalk with a determined, but wobbly, stride.

"Kasey, wait..." It was Dion. I wanted to stop. I wanted him to hold me. But I couldn't, and I sped up. I didn't look back. Then out of nowhere, I felt his grip on my forearm. He jerked me to a stop.

"Please. Let me help, or you will make yourself ill."

I wouldn't look at him. I began to cry. He pulled me close, and I collapsed burying my face in his chest.

"Everything will be alright," he said as he stroked my hair. I believed him. I believed his words.

After I stopped trembling he whispered, "Come, let us go somewhere and talk."

I let him take my hand and lead the way. My body didn't protest. I followed him willingly. We walked in silence until we came to a road that followed the cliff's edge. Between the road and the cliff, a three foot stonewall went for miles. We walked the road for a while and then sat on the wall. The crashing waves below us were loud, but calming. Inhaling and exhaling the air felt pure. I sat next to him. We both stared out across the water.

"Tell me what happened, Kasey," he said serious.

I recalled his brother lying dead on the forest floor. I didn't want to cry, "I must be crazy." My voice sounded distant even to me. Had I lost my voice?

He looked at me and smiled, "You are not crazy. I promise."

"You know what I saw, don't you?" I challenged.

"Why not tell me what you saw, and we will go from there."

Still uncertain, but wanting to trust him, I took a deep breath and explained what I had seen.

He interrupted before I finished, "Did you see any blood?"

"What?" I snapped.

"Did you see any blood?" he asked again in the same monotone voice.

I summoned up the memories of the gladiator fight. I tried to remember and realized he was right. It was a very clean scene, no blood.

"I don't understand how…" I whispered.

"Kasey, the world as you know it, is not what it seems." He stared across the ocean.

"What do you mean? What's going on Dion?" I demanded.

"Kasey, before I explain what you saw, there are a few things you need to know."

Where is he going with this?

He continued, "God does exist and oversees the heavens currently, but that was not always the case. Thousands of years ago, many gods once governed the heavens and Earth…"

"Dion are you going to tell me this is some kind of freakish religious thing!"

He rolled his eyes, "Simply hear me out. History as humans presumed happened is not entirely factual. Everything you think is a myth or legend, most likely happened."

"What are you talking about?" Was he trying to get out of explaining why his dead brother isn't dead?

"God created the Earth and all its inhabitants. However, after He created Earth and man spread throughout Earth's lands, God decided to leave for a while. In his place, He left his sons and daughters to reign above humans as Gods. Humans gave them various names; some refer to them as the Greek Gods."

I leaned back and crossed my arms over my chest then let out a huff.

He ignored me and continued, "As you know, there were numerous gods. They had the power to reproduce with each other and with mortals. They created many more gods and demigods. After time the heavens overcrowded with gods and goddess, so some left. In the end the only ones that truly remained to govern humans were the Olympians with their leaders Zeus, Hades, and Poseidon. I am sure you are somewhat studied in the area of Greek mythology?"

"Yea, somewhat, I read the Odyssey last year, what are you getting at?" I asked.

He chuckled, "Unfortunately, humans did not get all those facts right either. As Paganism was a popular belief system at the time, the gods were less than kind to humans who believed in the one God. So one day, as the Greeks refer to it, Chaos, or the one true God of us all, returned to Earth. He was appalled to see how his children's children were mistreating humans. He decided that He wanted full control over Earth again and demanded that all the gods step down and banished them from the heavens. The gods and goddess; were self-righteous and got extremely angry. They refused and declared war on the one true God. This is why God created his army of angels to battle the Greek gods. They battled in the heavens for thousands of years."

"Wait, are you telling me all those tales and stories are real, angels and gods do exist?" I couldn't believe he was feeding me some child's tale.

"Yes, they most certainly do exist. Finally, the one true God had enough. He knew the only way to win the battle was to have humans believe in Him and only Him. Therefore, He created his half-mortal son, the Christ child. He was the key, and even though the gods tried to stop his martyrdom; they failed. Jesus died, resurrected, and Christianity began. The war that started in the heavens now spread to Earth. Humans took sides; Paganism was destined to become extinct. As Christianity prevailed on Earth, the battle in the heavens was ending. The Greek gods and goddess surrendered to the one true God. God's archangels, led by Michael, gathered the Pagan gods for sentencing. The three leaders, Zeus, Poseidon, and Hades, vanished from Earth. The other gods had two choices, to leave Earth forever, or to live as an immortal with limited powers among humans. Most decided to stay. Any demigod or mortal who had direct interactions with the gods received the same fate. Most of them stayed on Earth."

"Are you telling me that your brother is an immortal Greek god?" I asked.

He smiled and half laughed, "No, we are immortal but we are not, nor ever were Greek gods."

"Excuse me...WE!"

"Yes, we, my brothers and I, we were born around two hundred years after Christ's resurrection. At this time, Christianity was still struggling against the Pagans on Earth. In the year 250 AD, my brothers and I were Ephesians, and at that time Artemis was the city's pagan goddess. The Roman Emperor Decius prosecuted Christians. When he came to Ephesus, he told us to pray to Artemis or die. Because we were the sons of a nobleman, he gave us a chance to ponder our decision. We were to tell him our choice upon his return. While he was away, my brothers and I climbed up a mountain and hid in a cave. We are not sure why or how exactly it happened, but we fell into a deep sleep."

"When the Emperor returned, he heard that we escaped to the mountain and were hiding in a cave. He had the mouth of the cave-sealed shut. My brothers and I lie sleeping in that cave for about one hundred and fifty years. Then one day the man who owned the land opened the mouth of the cave and we awoke. We had no idea what happened. Max went into the city to find out if the Emperor still wanted to persecute us. He was shocked to discover that there was a new Emperor, Christianity was the main religion, and it was one hundred and fifty years later."

I rubbed my eyes and shook my head. This couldn't be true. He's making up stories, isn't he?

## Men of the Cave

He sighed but continued, "Rumors and tales about us began to circulate the city. The Emperor summoned us to appear in front of him, and declared that our story was truth after investigating us. We were very popular and for what we did, were heroes of Christianity. We did not notice that we were not aging. About five years after our awakening, we realized we were not aging at all. We had to leave before people became suspicious. We faked our deaths and left the city. They canonized us as Saints. They call us the Seven Sleepers, even though we have never physically died. I know that the men we were, and the spirits we had been, before all this happened; are still buried in that city," he swallowed remembering something very painful.

"Seven Sleepers? There are only five of you." He has to be making this up.

"I have two other brothers. We parted ways a long time ago. We do not agree on how we should live our eternal lives," he said.

"What do you mean?"

"We five try to uphold good values. I can only say they walk a different path. As I said, we all buried the men we were. They often choose to misuse their powers."

"Whoa," I chuckled. "Powers?" He's just making it up as he goes.

"Ah, yes, I forgot to mention. Along with immortality we were given special abilities."

"Like what?"

"Max- Maximian can heal with his touch. Antony- Antoninos, can speak with animals. John- Joannes sees the future and Martin- Martinianus sees the past or present, but they can only do it when they focus together on an area or a person. Sam-Sambatus my older brother can leave his body in spirit form and move around in a ghost like way. James-Jamblichos my younger brother can move objects with his mind. Me-Dionysius, I am fast," he smiled.

My head started to throb. I closed my eyes.

"Are you all right Kasey?" he asked.

"I don't know Dion. Your story is the most outrageous thing I've ever heard. How can you possibly think I'd believe you?"

"Here I shall show you. I am so fast I can run on water."

He jumped into the ocean below us. I screamed after him, "Don't..." his body glided down like a kite and fell with a splash into the water. He swam slowly accelerating until he emerged, like a speedboat. As if running on dry land, he ran away from the rocks on top of the water. My heart pounded so hard I thought it would burst through my chest. I gripped the edge of the wall I was sitting on with all my might. He stopped for a second, turn, and headed back in my direction. Dion approached the rocks and like Spider Man climbed up the cliff in seconds. He sat beside me barely damp.

"What do you think?" he asked.

I looked at him. What is he? Can I trust my eyes? Or him?

"Kasey, you are looking at me as if I am some kind of a demon."

Men of the Cave

I didn't know what to think. The pressure in my head traveled down my body and through my arms. My view of Dion turned black and white, like an old movie. Sounds were distant and blurred. Then blackness.

## 7. Dion A Monster or A Knight

Thank goodness she fainted backwards so I could catch her in my arms, or that could have gotten tricky. Her body drained of color resembled a corpse. My stomach knotted. Lifting her close, I ran. The surrounding scenery sped by me as I passed at an accelerated speed. In a few seconds, I opened the red wooden door to our home.

"Maax...," I screamed, hoping my brothers were back at the house. Antony and John came out from the kitchen. Max and Martin raced down the stairs.

"Set her down," Max ordered.

I placed Kasey on the black leather sofa. Max's medical bag sat on the glass coffee table waiting for us. Martin and John had probably envisioned her here. I stepped back allowing Max the room he needed, but stayed close to her legs. His hand rose inches above her body, it illuminated with a bright yellow glow. Then he scanned her body like an x-ray machine.

"She will wake in a minute or so. Her blood sugar is low and her body went into shock. She needs to eat and drink something when she wakes," he stood.

"I shall bring her a plate of fruit," Antony headed for the kitchen.

"Thank you," I called out.

"What did you tell her?" Max asked serious.

"She knows," I answered.

"I cannot believe we were this careless." He looked at John and Martin. "Next time we need to make sure the grounds are secure," he ordered.

"We are sorry Max," Martin said.

"It is done. Dion can handle this." He folded his arms across his chest. "Call me when she wakes." He left toward the kitchen.

"He is really upset," John said.

"I wonder if it were someone other than Kasey, if he would have reacted the same way," I sighed.

"He will come around." John winked.

I smiled back at him, relieved. The twins headed for the game room. I threw myself onto the other sofa. Her fleshy color returned. She looked peaceful. I knew it was silly for me to worry, but what did she think of me, now? Every time I look at Kasey, I question whether I made the right choice to stay in Deia when John and Martin saw her in my future. Max suggested that I leave, running from my fate. How could I flee from the person God has intended for me? This unexplainable power and pull between us. I will never leave her now. The unbearable image of her haunted face before she fainted, tortured my thoughts. I was a monster to her, an unnatural being.

Kasey groaned and turned. Her eyes fluttered open. I stayed silent. A flicker of panic crossed her face when she realized her surroundings. She rose with a sudden pop. I went to her side and gently pushed her body back down, "You should not sit up quickly or you could faint again."

With an expression of concern, she did my bidding.

I smiled attempting to calm her. "How do you feel?"

She pondered the question.

"Where am I?" she asked in a hoarse voice.

"In my house, on my sofa." I sat on the coffee table across from her.

"I had the strangest dream. I think... you could walk on water."

I chuckled. "I did not walk on water."

She exhaled a sigh of relief.

"I ran."

Her eyes widened. Was she frightened of me? She shook her head and rubbed her temples.

"You need to eat something."

As if on cue, Antony and Max entered the room. Antony brought over a plate with assorted fruits and a glass of water.

"How long was I out?"

I held the plate in front of her. She ignored it.

"A few minutes, how are you feeling?" Max reached down, and lifted her wrist to monitor her pulse.

Her body stiffened. She tightened her arm to her side giving Max resistance. He ignored her. The wrinkles between her eyebrows pronounced, she looked uncomfortable. She didn't answer.

Max placed her wrist back down. "I would advise against getting up too soon. You need some water and food in your system. If you stand up you might collapse again. Rest here a few more minutes and eat something."

I met his eyes they furrowed.

"Thank you Max," I said.

He nodded then went upstairs, Antony followed. I offered Kasey the glass of water. She took it but still looked quite nervous. I placed my hand on her head and lightly rubbed her forehead with my thumb. She inched back at my approaching hand, and tensed her body from my touch. She removed my hand from her forehead.

"Try to relax no one is going to hurt you. I promise."

Kasey swallowed and her eyes glistened. She did not believe me.

"Here, please take some fruit."

She nodded but her hand trembled as she reached for an orange slice.

"Wh...what happened and how did I get here?" she whispered.

"You fainted after I showed you...well...my ability. I carried you here. Are you alright?"

"No!" She ate the orange and took a sip of water.

"Do you have any questions?" I asked.

"Questions! Of course I have questions! I just watched you run on water! I don't know what to think."

Her cheeks turned bright red. I placed my hand on her shoulder, and she allowed it.

"Please try to calm down. I will tell you anything you wish to know."

"What are you exactly?" She swung her legs down from the couch.

"An immortal."

"All immortals have special powers?"

"Yes."

"How many are there?" I saw the distress in her eyes.

"Many, but we do not have an exact number. There is no census for us. We tend to keep to ourselves."

She rubbed her eyes and let out a big sigh.

"What are you thinking?" I asked.

"You're extraordinary," she blurted.

"Oh, really!" I smiled.

"No I didn't mean it like that…I mean …well," she blushed and half smiled, "What I meant was this is extraordinary, it's unbelievable. You are like humans with super powers."

"Oh," I exaggerated an expression of disappointment.

"I think I should get home. I can't imagine what I'm going to tell the Castillo's," she said and grabbed a strawberry off the plate.

"Do not worry. Max spoke with them. They know you are here resting. We said you had a family issue that upset you and over worked your body."

"Still, I have to work tonight." She took a piece of tangerine.

"Of course. Whenever you are ready to go, I will be happy to take you."

She appeared calmer.

"Would you like a tour of the house?" I asked to test whether she could support herself on her feet.

Her eyes squinted, "I suppose I could."

I stood and reached my hand out. She failed to make eye contact with it, but took my offer. Carefully she stood.

I waited, "Are you light headed?"

"No... no I'm good." She stepped forward.

"I think the twins are in the game room."

I took her through our pristine kitchen that opened up to a room with no windows. Our game room consisted of a big flat screen TV with five black leather recliners. John and Martin stood in sword fighting positions playing Samurai Warrior on the game system.

"Kasey this is where John and Martin spend most of their time, normally."

The boys paused their game.

"You mean not out in a field sword fighting?" she asked.

They laughed, "You were not supposed to see that. That is the other thing we like to do." John said.

Uncertain, she stumbled on her words, "Wh...which one was murdered?"

"Murdered!" John repeated, amused. "Sounds violent."

"It was him." Martin pointed to John, "And I do not think the term murder applies."

"Martin usually loses." I chimed in.

"You will have to catch our re-match. It was my off day," John sulked.

"I have a question," Kasey began.

"Ask away," I said.

"Why did he pretend to be dead?"

"When we get stabbed through the heart by a blade our bodies are immobilized. Our spirits stay trapped in our bodies until the sword is out. Only when the blade pierces through our hearts do we lay dormant otherwise the blade does not affect us. Our bodies instantly heal back to normal," Martin answered.

"That is how I knew. I was dormant but still aware within my body. I saw you approach me and could do nothing. Martin left me there to get some water…"

"Hey, you did the same thing to me last week. At least I didn't wait ten minutes to pull it out." Martin shoved his brother's shoulder.

John continued ignoring him, "As soon as he returned and pulled the sword from my chest we came to find you." John shook his head.

"It is our only weakness, we cannot die or get hurt, but we can be trapped until we are freed." I let her know.

"Do you feel any pain?" Kasey wondered.

"Yes, we feel the pain, but only briefly," I answered.

"Not that you would really know," John grumbled.

"What does he mean?" she asked.

"Dion is the best. It is difficult to defeat him in a duel, due to his speed," Martin spoke well of me.

"Interesting," she smirked. "How old were you guys when you died?"

"John and Martin are forever fifteen, I am twenty, Antony is twenty three, and Max is twenty-five." I answered.

"What about the other two brothers?"

I let out a big sigh, "Sam is twenty one and James is seventeen."

"Don't people notice that you don't age?"

"Good Lord, she is going to be a billion questions for the next few weeks. Good luck Dion." John plopped into his recliner.

"I'm sorry, I have so many," she said.

"It is quite all right, I expected as much." I gestured for us to exit the room.

"If you have any more you want to ask me Kasey, catch me some other time and I shall fill you in." Martin offered. The boys resumed their game.

She followed me out.

"Would you like to go upstairs?" I did not want to take her home, yet. She walked by the coffee table and grabbed the plate of fruit, "Sure."

"Would you like anything else? I could find something in the kitchen?"

"Nope this is fine." She followed me upstairs.

Our second floor consisted of a t-shaped hallway with six bedrooms equal in size. We started to pass the first two rooms.

"What room is this?" Kasey asked as she entered the battle area.

"This is our weapons room." I answered following her. "We have all types of swords, daggers, arrows, and shields in here from various time periods. Most are authentic."

"No kidding," she muttered under her breath. "Do you all battle like gladiators?"

"Yes, it was the 'in' thing to do when we were living. We enjoy sparing. It helps to know you cannot hurt your opponent."

"You don't consider yourself to be alive now?" This confused her.

"To live is to die. We are incapable of dying therefore we are not truly alive either."

"Interesting, what do you like to fight with?"

"I like dagger fighting. You have to be quick with sharp movements. This one, the mid first century Roman Pugio Dagger is my preference."

Taking the fourteen-inch long dagger off the wall, I slide it out of its iron-plated sheath. Then I swung it in fancy circles and laid it out in front of her so that she could hold it. Kasey took the sword with gentle hands. She treated it as if she were going to break it.

"It's light," she said.

"It weighs two pounds."

"Tell me about it," she asked.

"The blade is an hour glass shaped metal with a sharp tip. There are engraved lines that run from the tip to the edge of the grip handle. The handle is metal coated with gold. The t-shaped handle has a ball at the end inlaid with rubies and emeralds. In the middle of the part you grip you can see a lion engraved into the gold."

"It's beautiful." She admired the intricate details on the handle.

"It is the dagger that killed Julius Caesar," I mentioned coolly.

"Uh…you mean this type of dagger is the kind that killed him, right?"

"No, I mean that is actually one of the blades that went through his body."

The complete petrified look on Kasey's face alarmed me.

"Take it! Take it!" she squealed.

I took it quickly and placed it back in its sheath.

"Are you mad? Why isn't that in a museum? I can't believe you have this. You mean this actually killed Julius Caesar?"

"Yes, we take pleasure in collecting rare and valuable items. Since we are time travelers, we tend to have an advantage over human archeologists. We have relics all around the world in our different houses. That is how we are wealthy. We barter and sell antiques."

"How many houses do you have?" she asked, astonished.

"Twenty-seven."

"Oh my God! How did you get the dagger that killed Julius Caesar? Wasn't that before your time?"

She impressed me by her knowledge of history. "We met once a descendant of Caesar who hid the dagger amongst their belongings. This person discovered our truth and since we could live forever they sold it to us for a hefty price, so that we could preserve it."

"This is incredible. I would love to see the artifacts you have."

"Perhaps one day we will go and see all of my twenty-seven houses," I flirted. She blushed and turned from me.

"Come on let us go see Max."

She stepped out the door. As I turned off the lights, I heard her gasped from the hallway. Immediately, I stepped out to her. She stood like an ancient Greek statue.

"Dion!" She screeched in a whispered voice.

Layna, Antony's black panther strutted down the hallway.

"Oh, that is Layna. She is Antony's friend. She has made herself at home with us."

Layna stopped in front of us and looked at Kasey.

"Layna this is Kasey, she is a friend of mine."

Kasey looked at me as if I were mad. Layna shook her head.

Antony came around the corner. "She says your mad Dion if you think the human is going to pet her like a pussy cat."

Kasey looked at Antony astounded.

"Really. She is capable of that type of higher level thinking?"

Layna let out a puff of air, and then walked down the stairs. Antony snickered.

"What did she say?" Kasey asked.

"Oh, brother," Antony replied with a smile.

"Kasey, Layna is not a pet. She is literally a friend. Animals are similar to humans," I said.

"Layna is one of the most gifted feline minds I have ever met. She and I got along instantly. I met her in South America, and she was utterly bored with her mundane jungle life. I offered her to come with us and she has been a friend of the family ever since. We could not get rid of her even if we tried." Antony explained then followed Layna downstairs.

"That's unbelievable." Kasey shook her head.

"You will find that most things in the immortal world are." I showed her the way to Max's room. He was at his desk. As a good mannered gentlemen would, he put down his medical book and stood to greet us.

"How are you feeling Kasey?" Max asked.

"I'm all right thank you."

"Would you mind if I see for myself?" He asked and took a step closer to Kasey.

She stiffened and glared at me as if I had betrayed her.

"I'm fine, really."

"All I will do is wave my hand in front of you, to make sure. I do not need to touch you I promise." He showed her his hand palm out.

She nodded but her shoulders lifted and her hands made fists. Max's hand glowed as he waved it over her body like a scanner. Kasey's jaw dropped, her eyes fixed on his hand.

"Your vitals are back to normal. You should not run on an empty stomach. It is not a good idea. If you are careless again you could faint once more," he said and stopped his exam.

"Yeah... cause that's what made me faint." She replied with sarcasm.

Max did not like her response he folded his arms across his chest. There was an apparent awkwardness between them.

"This should have never happened," he said.

"You don't have to worry. It's not like I'm going to tell anyone," Kasey retorted.

"I know you will not. People would think you are mad. No one would believe you," Max said monotone.

"Well...um..." Kasey looked at me for help.

"Kasey needs to get back. Thank you again Max. I will stay with her until dinner. What time would you like to meet up tonight?" I asked.

He narrowed his eyes. "Do you think it is wise? I thought we could go to Palma tonight to eat." He always tried to keep me from her.

Kasey gave me a strange look. "Um, you chaps can go. I think I am going to stick around town. *Valete*."

We walked out of the room.

"What's *valete*?" Kasey asked.

"Latin for good bye."

"Is Max angry that I know your secret?" she asked.

"Yes. It is an unspeakable law that humans are not to know of our existence. Sometimes accidents happen." I sneered at her.

Kasey stopped in the middle of the hallway. She looked around. "Where's your room?"

"Do you not have to get back promptly?" I did not want her to see my room.

She eyed me warily. "Nope, I think I have time to see your room."

"Ah… some other day."

"Why?"

Something told me, she was not going to let me get out of this.

"I am not the tidiest person."

"It's okay; I'm not going to look at the mess. I don't care," she urged.

"You cannot miss it. It is the door across from Max's," I said hesitant.

She headed for the mahogany door and walked in.

"Holy shit!"

I lowered my head and followed her in.

"Yes, I know, it is a mess."

She chuckled, "You are such an oddity. Why are their piles of cloths everywhere?"

She walked around the room.

"It is how I organize my clothes. See this pile is my clean colored cloths. That one is my dirty light colored cloths. These are the ones that need to go to a dry cleaner…"

"Why don't you put them away?"

"I hate putting cloths away. I do a lot of ironing because of it. But who is going to change a two thousand year old habit." I plopped onto my bed.

"The room is decorated with an Astronomical theme. Do you like Astronomy?" she asked.

"Yes, I love the stars. We have a big telescope on the roof. I shall take you up there sometime."

"Hmmm… all twenty-seven houses and to the roof to see the telescope. Seems like you're going to have to take me many places," she teased.

"I would show you the world if you wished." I enjoyed our line of conversation.

"Interesting the world could be fun. Perhaps someday I will take you up on that."

"In due time, my dear," I replied.

Her demeanor changed and it seemed like some type of light turned on in her head.

"Did John have any future visions of me?" she asked with a hint of suspicion in her voice. I sat up and got serious. What do I tell her? The truth or can I lie.

"Yes."

"When?" she asked.

Why did she have to ask me this?

"The first day we heard you were coming to Deia and after you and I were conversing by the ocean," I answered.

"Wait, before you even met me?"

"Yes."

"What did John see?" she asked again.

"Kasey, maybe we should…"

She interrupted me. "Dion, I have a right to know. Good or bad, what did he see?"

Hesitant and ill feeling, I answered. "He saw us…and you…you told me you loved me." I murmured the words.

Her jaw dropped and her eyes stood still in shock. This was as uncomfortable for her as it was for me. How could she see this coming?

"Oh, um..." She turned bright red. "I don't know what to say."

"There is nothing you have to say. Let me take you home now?" I stood from the bed. I wanted nothing more than to give her a reassuring hug, but I held back.

"I think that's a great idea," she whispered.

We walked into the hall, down the stairs, out the front door, and into my Mini Cooper in utter silence. When we reached the end of the driveway she spoke again, "How much of what John sees comes true?"

"All of it." I looked straight at the road.

"So fate is predestined no matter what?" she asked in disbelief.

"Yes."

"Oh..." She did not like my reply. "Dion, What did Martin see?"

"The first time he saw a man."

"What man?"

"Martin described him as being our age with curly dirty blonde hair and tan."

Based on her expression I thought she recognized the man I was describing.

"Kasey, let me explain John and Martin's abilities, and perhaps you can better deal with their visions. In the beginning, after we awoke from our sleep, they struggled. They were unable to control the visions and an attack happened at any minute. They would get visions of death all the time. It took us many years of working together to try to help them learn how to keep it under control."

"Now, they rarely get a spontaneous vision, only if someone close to them is in danger, or a major event is about to happen. For the most part, they can summon up what they wish to see. For example Elena Castillo, we are close to her family and were close to her. The minute she got into the car Martin and John received their visions. Even so, we were still too late. It is not a perfected science. For a few years, they decided to work with the police. Focusing on the crime scene, they could see how the murder happened and where the killer was hiding. They did not do that for too long. All the death got to them. With you, because of your…well your…future connection to me, the mention of your name gave them an instant vision."

"Dion, about what they saw for me…"

"Kasey wait, before you go on any further let me say this. I have been accustomed to their fortunetelling for hundreds of years. The best advice I can give is this, yes, fate will happen the way it is intended, but it is not going to ensue sooner than meant to. Even though John sees the future, the future must happen in its right place in time. It is impossible to speed it up. Do you understand this?" I parked the car in front of el Restaurante Caracoles.

"I understand. I think." As fast as she could she opened the car door and got out. I raced with my ability to meet her before she entered the restaurant. With a gentle grip, I held her forearm.

"Are you alright?" I asked.

Kasey forced a smile. "Yeah, of course." She looked away. She was lying.

She leaned up and kissed my cheek.

I released my hold on her and she entered the restaurant.

## 8. Kasey and Destiny

"Kasey, he is so hot! We are going dancing tonight in Palma. Would you like to come?" Madhu and I shared a big bowl of Catalan cream at *el Restaurante* Caracoles. She had stopped by for lunch and we were finishing desert.

"I'm sorry, Madhu, but correct me if I'm wrong. Aren't you engaged?"

"No, I am betrothed. Not the same thing. Plus how could I pass up this beautiful Italian bombshell that moved into my building?" She had an exaggerated way about her.

"Are you allowed to see other men knowing that you are supposed to marry some guy back in Bangladesh?"

"Yes, I do not have to marry until we are both finished with school. I can see other people as long as I remember not to get too close. If I get too close, I leave."

I shook my head. "I can't believe you."

"I do not have to worry about my parent's watchful eyes over here. I am going to explore as much as I can before I have to play housewife for the rest of my life."

We spoke in depth on the subject of arranged marriages. I never understood how calm she was about the whole thing. She accepted it as part of her culture, and it wasn't a big deal. Madhu found it amusing that the whole concept would irritate me. I was willing to go to war with her parents and battle this backward notion. She didn't want any of that. She liked the guy she was supposed to marry, and they knew each other since they were kids.

"So, Kasey will you come out dancing in Palma tonight?" She questioned a second time.

I shrugged my shoulders. "Sure, that might be fun."

She took another spoonful of cream. "Why not call Dion, and ask him to come?"

"Hmmm..." I shook my head no and took another serving of cream.

"How long has it been since you guys have spoken?"

"Three weeks."

"Kasey, why not call him?"

"I got my license and Fernando helped me rent a car. I don't need him to drive me anymore. He was someone who did something nice for me nothing more." I played with the silver spoon. I avoided the Kleon family as if they were a nest of snakes. They didn't come every night to the restaurant like before. I suspected they respected my wishes and stayed away.

"Well, that is the biggest bull I ever heard," she said.

"What?"

"Come on Kasey anyone could see you two connected. I do not know what happened, but it has bothered you all these weeks. You know you want to talk to him. Call him, and invite him to go dancing."

"What do you mean we connected?"

"Kasey it was obvious. You two are disgustingly adorable. I shall see you both tonight." She smiled and stood to go.

"Madhu…I …don't think…" The cream sat heavy.

"Bernando and I will pick you both up at ten thirty." With that, she left the restaurant.

After clearing the dishes, I went upstairs to find Garcia sitting in front of a chess board. He was staring at the pieces scattered as if they were in play.

"What are you doing?" I broke his concentration.

"I like to practice. My father is quite good, and one day I shall defeat him."

I loved how close the Castillos were. Garcia always looked after Rodrigo and never complained about it. They enjoyed each other's company. Fernando and Beatriz were model parents, the kind I never had. Their only fault was that the restaurant took too much of their private time, so it left them with little free time. That's why I think the boys were so close. The whole family willingly helped with the family business, even Catalina. There was no question where their priorities lie. I sat down across from Garcia and asked, "Want to play a short round?"

"Short," he asked confused. "Chess is not short," he informed me.

"Well, against me, I bet it will be the quickest game you ever won." I placed the pieces in the starting position.

His eyes lit up, "Let us play then."

As we moved our pawns one at a time I said, "Tell me about Catalina. How was she before?"

I wanted to be cautious and not bring up anything that would be too sad for him to relive.

"She was a weirdo, but not this strange. She and Elena were close. Like Rodrigo and I. I think Elena kept her a little normal. So when she passed, Catalina lost it." He shrugged and moved another pawn.

"How did you do that?" His pawns progressed. "Does she hate Americans because of Elena's boyfriend?"

"Yes, she thinks Americans are reckless and don't care about anyone. But you are not like that Kasey, you are very nice." He reminded me of my little brother, they were the same age. Garcia blushed slightly and took another knight from me.

We played for about an hour, and he pulverized me. After our game, he went to help downstairs, and I headed for my room. Every day I checked my phone about ten times waiting for Dion's number to pop up. It hadn't. What would I say to him? How am I supposed to ask him to go dancing when we haven't spoken in three weeks? He might not even come.

Would his brothers have told him I would be calling? Was I to go out with him tonight? I stood in front of my desk with my phone in hand. I found his number, then I put the phone down and sat on my bed. If I call him would I be setting into motion a chain of predestined events? Then again, am I being over analytical? I did miss his chats. My gut feeling screamed danger, warning. Then again, I have always been attracted to things I shouldn't. I walked over to the phone and pressed the talk button.

It rang once, please let it go to voice mail, it rang twice, three times. "How have you been Kasey?" His deep, lyrical voice came through.

I let out the breath I was holding. Why did he have to pick up?

"I'm ...I'm good and you?"

"I have been well. So, you can drive. What car did you rent?"

"A Suzuki Jimny. It's nice, but it's no Mini Cooper."

He laughed, "I knew you had a good sense about you when it came to cars."

I envisioned his alluring smile.

"Yeah, I was calling because Madhu, some guy she met, and I are going dancing tonight in Palma. We wanted to know if you would like to go."

He snickered, "We...huh...sounds like fun. I would love to go out on a date tonight."

I cringed at his comment. He knew! I bet he knew I would call.

"Okay...yeah...um... they are going to be here at ten thirty."

"Not a problem. If it is all right, could I arrive early? Would ten fifteen work?"

"That's fine."

"See you then." He said and clicked the phone off.

I let out a huge sigh. That went oddly well. I couldn't believe that I called him. Now, how do I get the nerve to go out on a date? My anxiety level rose. I worried about his expectations. Did he think of me as the perfect woman predestined for him? What if he's disappointed? We are so different, yet there was something about our differences, I couldn't resist. My thoughts were driving me crazy. If I was going out late, I needed a nap. The drowsiness, quietness, and the stillness of the room lent itself to the perfect afternoon siesta.

******

A few hours later, I awoke feeling refreshed. I jumped into the shower for a rapid wash. Standing in front of my armoire, I faced the most difficult choice of the night. What do I wear? I wasn't exactly the clubbing type and my wardrobe definitely did not lend itself to the occasion. What would he be wearing? More importantly, what would he like to see me wear? Did he like the short skirt and string tops that girls normally wore to clubs?

He's two thousand years old. What kind of woman would someone like him want? I grabbed all my skirts and threw them on my bed. Then I grabbed the sexiest night appropriate tops and began my wardrobe debacle. After many attempts, I went back into my armoire and pulled out my only special occasion outfit. My mid-thigh ivory slip with a detailed lace overlay. The sleeves flared out at my elbows. The dress belonged to my father's mother, Adora. She passed away when he was young. I let my curls fall free and slid on my white knee-high leather boots.

Wrapped up in getting ready, I lost complete track of time. The knock on my door came as a surprise. Was he here already? I picked up my phone and sure enough, the numbers read ten fifteen. Crap, I went over to the door.

"Hi. Impeccable timing," I said. He was dressed in a shimmery black shirt and white slacks. Dion looked flawless.

"I am usually punctual. You look stunning." He smiled, leaned forward, and tried to peck my cheek. Nervous, I stepped back, so that he couldn't. He sighed disappointed.

"Thank you. I wasn't sure what to wear." I turned from him into my room.

"Good choice. What happened in here? It looks as bad as my room." He viewed my clutter.

"This doesn't even come close to that bad," I said closing the door. "I have a few things to finish up. Make yourself at home. Where ever you can." I walked into the bathroom but left the door opened in case he wanted to talk.

"So," his voice came through the crack, "How have you been, Kasey?"

"Good." I left it at that. I began to apply my eyeliner.

"Just good? Last time we talked…well…we had an interesting day."

"That's putting it mildly."

"I must admit I am pretty surprised that you did not call earlier. I thought you had many questions. Then when you do call you invite me out on a date."

"Whoa…we are just going dancing with other people. This was Madhu's idea." I said, coming out of the bathroom.

He sat on my desk chair with a very sexy grin. My cheeks blushed.

"Dancing, with another couple, it sounds to me like a double date. But call it as you wish."

I huffed.

"I...I don't know why I didn't call Dion. I guess it was all overwhelming and I was nervous."

"Nervous? You have nothing to be nervous about. Are you afraid of me?" This seemed to bother him.

"I don't know you... you aren't typical..."

"I can be typical. Are we not going on a typical date scenario tonight? Kasey, treat me like you would any ordinary American boy..."

"Dion, there is nothing ordinary about you. Plus, I feel pressured. I can't imagine what your expectations are..."

Before I could finish, he stood before me. He placed his hands around my elbows. Then he slid them down until my hands were in his. I allowed his touch. I let out a small sigh and looked away from him. My heart hit the inside of my chest with violent pounds. On the back of my neck, a tingly sensation started and worked its way down my spine.

"Kasey, I have no expectations. Please, stop worrying. I enjoy your company and if you find my company enjoyable, then let us focus on the here and now. Try not to think about my differences. We shall attempt to have a good time tonight."

I nodded. "Did Martin and John have a vision?" I stared into his dark eyes.

He smiled. "Yes."

"How's tonight going to end?"

"I do not know. I told them not to tell me unless there was something dangerous that would occur."

I narrowed my eyes. "Really?"

"Yes, I want tonight to be a complete and total surprise." He squeezed my hands twice.

"I bet your definition of dangerous is completely different from mine."

He laughed.

The chime from my phone interrupted our moment. It rang once and stopped.

"That's Madhu, she downstairs," I whispered.

"Are you ready?" he asked.

"Yes…yes I am." I swallowed nervously. I grabbed my phone, my little black purse, and my thin sweater, then we left.

Madhu and Bernardo sat in a silver convertible Peugeot. Bernardo stayed seated behind the driver's seat. Madhu opened the door and got out to let us into the back.

"*Hola*," she said and gave me a kiss on my cheek.

"You look cute," I grinned. She wore a black sweater over a silver beaded sparkly top with a black tight mini jean skirt.

"*Gracias*, you too. Great to see you, Dion." By the look on her face, she wasn't sure I was really going to call him. I stepped into the backseat of the car.

We said our greetings then were on our way. Bernardo was semi-attractive in a Fabio type of way. His dark features complimented his coal black shoulder length hair pulled back into a ponytail. The late Spain air was crisp and cool in the convertible. I shivered a few times. Dion put his arm around me. I didn't fight it or pull away. I welcomed the warmth and desired the closeness.

Everything was going to change tonight. The future was set into motion. I closed my eyes and inhaled the salty air. The romantic Mediterranean atmosphere, the magical city, and a world filled of immortals with super powers I was going to let the universe bring a night of possibilities my way.

## 9. Kasey and the Mermaid

The city shone in the night like a million glowworms sitting out in a meadow. Alive, it bustled with people and cars coming out to party. The club that Madhu and Bernardo chose was perfect, *La Sirena*, the mermaid an outdoor nightclub right on the bay. The clear blue-lit dance floor sat over the ocean water. The bar and the tiny shell tables were all themed to the clubs name. The D.J. played Latin music. Like seaweed dancing under water, beautiful people moved on the dance floor.

"How do you like it, Kasey?" Madhu screamed as we grabbed an available high top with four stools.

"This is very cool, I love the atmosphere." I yelled back.

Bernardo leaned into Madhu's ear, and they giggled together. Dion's hand tickled my ear as he placed my hair behind it, "What would you like to drink?" he asked.

"I don't know, something light, simple."

The music blared. In order to hear each other we kept our faces close. His baby soft skin and warm breath tingled every pore on my cheek.

"I will be back."

Bernardo took Dion's lead and made his way toward the bar as well.

Madhu scooted over to me. "Sooo, you and Dion seem chummy with each other. What happened when you called?"

"He said yes, and we are going to see how it goes tonight," I said making light of the whole thing.

"If he tries to kiss you, you let him. Take my advice." Madhu shook her finger at me.

"What?"

"It is all revealed in the kiss. If he tries, let him. You will know by the kiss."

"Know what?" I asked, but the men returned and we focused our attention to them.

"Thank you," I said taking a sip of sweet white wine. "It's good."

"Glad you like it," he said. "It is a two thousand and nine white Chivite."

That meant nothing to me but obviously something to him.

"The wine will keep you warm."

The night had a brittle cool breeze.

"Ready to dance?"

"Let me guess you're a great dancer, right?" I asked.

"Of course," he said cocky. After two thousand years of living, I assumed cockiness was something naturally developed.

I held my own on the dance floor, but his expertise level surpassed mine. He was patient and great at taking the lead. Even though I looked like a baby bird flapping its wings for the first time, he made me feel like I was a twirling floating snowflake.

We would dance, take breaks with some more sips of wine, and then continue dancing. After one glass of wine, I began to feel loopy and had a hard time on the dance floor. Dion twirled me around fast and the world spun dizzily for a few seconds. He jerked me to a stop and grabbed my arm.

"Are you okay?" he screamed over the music.

I shook my head no. "I think the wine has gotten to me." I fanned myself.

He helped me to the table. "I will fetch you some water."

I tried to focus on a non-moving object. The whirling impression in my head caused my slight dizziness. My stomach began to cramp and I had this strange sensation, an awkward feeling as if something important was to happen. I spotted Madhu and Bernardo having a great time on the dance floor.

On the other side of the club, two dark haired men sat at a table staring at me. They didn't look like Spaniards, they were foreign. They had an heir of familiarity, but I couldn't place their ethnicity. They didn't look away when I caught them gawking. They wore serious stern expressions. The young men made me uneasy. I looked away. Their faces suggested that I was in some way bothering them. I couldn't help myself, I looked back in their direction and they were gone.

"How are you feeling? Is something wrong?" Dion returned with a glass of water.

I shook my head. "Nothing, I think I became tipsy and the twirling made it worse."

"No more wine then."

By two o'clock I was hungry and tired. Mahdu and Bernardo decided they wanted to go to another place before heading home.

"Are you sure you do not wish to come with us?" Madhu asked reconfirming.

"No, no we are okay. I want to get back to Deia. Don't worry, we will hail a cab." I reassured her with a goodbye hug.

"All right Kasey, *adios*." She leaned into my ear. "And good luck." Madhu winked before she got into the convertible with Bernardo. They drove off and I turned to face Dion.

"So, what are you hungry for?" he asked.

"I don't know. I think I'm too tired to eat. I want to get back to Deia. I can get something there if I'm still hungry."

"I know a couple of sandwich shops open this late. How do you want to get home?"

"Well, I was thinking a cab. Why?"

"How fast do you want to get home? I am quicker than a cab."

"Are you serious? You could carry me all the way to Deia running!"

"Yes."

"Um…Dion I'm not exactly the lightest person…"

"Kasey please, you are practically a feather to me."

"Well…um…okay let's give this a try." Nervous I looked around.

He laughed, "Not here, too public. Let us take a walk down toward the beach where it is more deserted. Then from there I can run."

"Right… gotcha."

His fingers softly slipped into mine and he led the way. The beach was not far an eight-minute walk or so.

"You surprised me tonight, Kasey. You are a decent dancer."

"Thank you. How is it that you seem to be an expert at almost everything?"

"Years of practice."

"Tell me…about that."

"About what exactly?" He was tender.

"I don't know…how about the Greek gods that now live on Earth."

"There are a lot of them, I know some. We are good friends with a few demigods. They are scattered around the world. I am surprised that only a few of us are in Deia right now."

"Wait, what do you mean by that?" I asked.

"Deia is a special place where immortals can come and stay for a longer time. We never have to worry about questions. The people here just look the other way at us. Take Helena for example, she has never left this little village. She says it brings her peace after the life she endured."

"Wait, Helena? The old woman she's immortal?"

"Yes, she is Helen of Troy the demigod," he said casually.

I stopped walking.

"You mean I have met the Helen of Troy and she made me lunch," I whispered my words.

"Yes, but do not believe all the stories you have been taught, humans embellish and exaggerate a lot." He stopped with me.

Awe struck I stared into the dark water.

"How could you not tell me who she was?"

"Kasey, at the time you did not know about our world."

"I can't believe that was Helen of Troy. Why is she an old woman and blind?"

"She chose that form when she was sentenced by God. She wanted to spend the rest of her immortal life not being desired by men or even to look at them." He continued to walk I followed.

"Does she have a special power?" I asked.

"Yes, she can read your thoughts when she touches your face. God graced her with that because she cannot see."

"Really… did she read mine?" Mildly concerned I couldn't remember what I was thinking when we met.

"Yes," he smiled.

"Ohhhh… that wasn't nice. You tricked me by taking me there."

"No, it was no trick. I needed to stop by to pick up lunch. It was a coincidence that you were with me and met her." He strained to sound legitimate.

I didn't buy it. "Uh-hum, sure. What did she tell you?" Suddenly alarmed, I feared I thought something about him and didn't even know it. He snickered and turned to face the ocean. Whatever it was, it was going to embarrass me.

"Dion! How awful what did she say?" I placed my hand on his shoulder I turned him toward me.

"Nothing awful," he laughed.

"Tell me! What did she say?" My temper escalated.

"I do not want you to be upset." He avoided the question.

"So, tell me what she told you! Or I will be upset!" I was seconds from exploding.

He looked down with a sly grin, "You really think I could have my own photo shoot."

I stopped breathing. My hands covered my face. "Oh, God," I whispered.

He wrapped his arms around me and brought me close into him. "Do not fret about this. I thought it was adorable."

I removed my hands from my face. "That was not nice. How could you do that to me? Those thoughts are private."

"I am sorry, please do not be angry," he said in a puppy dog way. I pushed back from his embrace and resumed our walk. He followed.

"If she has been living there all these centuries does this mean that the village knows the truth?"

"I think they know some people are unique, they pass the information from generation to generation. The best part is they never question."

We reached the deserted beach.

"What if someone sees us?" I asked concerned about the stunt we were minutes from pulling off.

"I shall be going too fast for anyone to notice. Moreover, I am careful. I take deserted roads. Once we are out of the city it is all country until Deia. No one will be able to see us."

"Okay, let's do this. What do you want me to do?"

"Nothing, I am going to pick you up like this." He picked me up and cradled me like a baby. I wrapped my arms around his neck.

"Ready," he whispered.

"Ready," I whispered back.

Dion ran. The wind hit my face. It was forceful and I felt like an astronaut taking off into space. It was impossible to open my eyes. I had no other choice than to bury my face into his shoulder. The ride lasted a minute at most. He stopped, and squeezed me closer. He was warm and cozy. I could smell the deep aromas of his after-shave, musk on a moonlit beach. I inhaled and exhaled.

"Are you all right?" he asked.

I managed to detach myself from his chest. "Are we here?" I looked around.

"Yes, this is the back of my house."

"That was intense. How fast were we going?"

"A fifth of a mile per second."

"How long did it take?" I was astounded.

"Two minutes, I can go five times the speed of sound, but I did not go nearly that fast because of you," he boasted.

"How are you able to see?"

"I am not sure. The pressure does not affect me."

"You can put me down now."

"Of course. Sorry."

I put my outfit back into place due to the high-speed winds from the run.

"Remind me if we ever do that again not to wear a dress."

He grinned and his eyes glanced down toward his feet. "I tried to keep your dress in place. I was afraid it was going to blow up."

"Yea, I felt that."

The placement of his hand had shifted to my thigh after he began the run. Even with the dim moon light, I could tell he blushed. He turned away embarrassed. Adorable, the moon's light merely helped accent his god given splendid features.

"So, your house?" I questioned suspiciously.

"I thought I could show you the telescope, if you wished. If not, we can do something else. Anything you desire Kasey."

My brow raised, "Careful with those words, Dion."

"What do you have in mind?"

"Telescope's fine."

I removed my boots to walk across the sand, and we made our way to the wooden staircase that went up to the cliff's edge. When we reached the top, we stopped in front of a dimly lit walking path into the dark forest.

"I don't get it. With the amazing view of the ocean why would you cover it up with a forest?" I hesitated. I didn't care for the shadowy path.

"It lends itself to more privacy. The house is elevated you can still see the ocean from it. The walkway goes up some more."

"Are there any living creatures in there? It's pretty dark." I regretted removing my boots.

"Not really, maybe a big spider or snake is the worse you will find." He took my reluctant hand and pulled me along. I grabbed on to his arm and hugged it tight. I shuffled my feet in low quick movements.

"Kasey, what are you doing?"

"If there are snakes around, you shuffle your feet to scare them away."

He started laughing. "You silly girl." He reached down, picked me up, and cradled me in his arms. Our faces were inches from each other.

"There, now the snakes will not get you," he whispered.

"Thank you," I replied. We held our pose. His pupils danced. Did he want a kiss? He tilted his head ever so slowly toward me and I turned my head away. I didn't care if destiny intended for us to be together, I wasn't ready to feel another boy's lips on mine. Even if it was Dion's.

"Can't you do your speedy thing and get us to the house quicker? Something about forests at night makes me uncomfortable."

He sighed, "The path is not that long. I do not think I have to use my abilities to get us to the house."

## 10. Kasey and the Brothers

It really was just ahead thank goodness. He put me down as soon as we came to the paved clearing. The back of the Kleon house looked like a paradise vacation resort.

"Oh, this is beautiful."

The deck area was a three level stone floor beauty. The lowest level, the one the path let out to, had a gorgeous, oddly shaped, pool with a stoned waterfall trickling into it. Green florescent lights lit up inside the pool. Lined along the spa's edge were enormous stone pots with greenery in them. On either side of the spa two, gigantic ivory bowls with tall flames extended high into the air. The house sat on the third deck level. The second floor was dark except for the spotlights over the balcony. On the first floor, a light came from the right three sliding glass doors.

"How odd…it is two o'clock in the morning. Why are my brothers up?" Dion headed for the light. I had hoped to put my boots on but he gave me no time. A light came from the living room. Several dark shadows could be seen, some standing others sitting.

# Men of the Cave

When we entered, everyone in the room stopped and looked at us. Max glared disapprovingly. John checked me out, nodded, then smiled favorably. A petite, dark-skinned man wearing a tan suit and small glasses sat on the sofa. Sweating too much for any normal human, he appeared anxious. Was he a Greek god or another type of god? He passed a handkerchief over his forehead.

"What is going on?" Dion seemed alarmed.

I stayed back in the shadows. The man in the tan suit caught sight of me and stood. He said something in a language, I did not recognize. Then he pointed at me. All the brothers looked my way, and I wished for a turtle's shell so that I could make myself disappear. My stomach cramped again. That familiar sensation tingled all over my body. Something serious was to happen, and soon.

"She is a friend of mine, Kassandra Reese." Dion replied to the man in English.

The man looked me up and down.

"Is she immortal?" he asked with a British accent.

"No," Max answered.

"Well, I have never... what is her lineage?" The man kept prying.

"I don't think I understand. I don't know my lineage," I said. "Why do you want to know?"

"My dear...the similarity between you and Pandora is astounding." He wiped his forehead.

I looked at the man, then to Dion, and back at the strange man. That's the second person that's mentioned I look like Pandora. What was going on here?

"Kasey, this is Professor Darius Mubarak, an Egyptologist from Cairo. You know, Professor, you are not the first person to mention her likeness to Pandora. Helen did when she first met her."

Whoa, are they actually saying that I'm related to one of their kind? This can't be happening!

"How? Immortals are incapable of breeding." The Professor shook his head, wiped his forehead, then sat. "I would like to take a blood sample from her and compare it to Pandora's DNA back at my lab."

What does he want?

"You have Pandora's DNA?" Max asked suspiciously.

"I have a lot of immortal's DNA. You are a fascinating breed. For years, I have been trying to figure out how you heal. I would like to take Ms. Reese's blood and cross-reference it to Pandora. If Pandora is breeding, then I think we ought to look into it."

"Fine, I shall get it for you before you leave," Max huffed.

My eyes grew wide. I turned to Dion.

He whispered, "Is that all right?"

"No!" I whispered back. "They can't just have my blood."

"All they are going to do is check to see if you are related to Pandora. It will be fine, trust me."

I nodded, but remained unsure. Suddenly, I wished I'd never gone on this date.

"Professor this is not why you came to Deia at two in the morning, is it?" Dion changed the tone of the conversation.

"Professor, please inform Dion of our earlier conversation. I shall be right back," Max headed upstairs.

"It is about Sam and James, Dion. I think they are on their way here to kill you." The Professor wiped his brow.

"What? That is impossible…"

"No, it might not be. They came to me two days ago for a translation. They uncovered a tablet created by Zeus before he banished. On that tablet there is a curse. And it says if you recite the curse before slaying an immortal with a steel blade through the heart, they will die. The slayer inherits the dead man's special ability." The Professor said anxious.

"Do you think this tablet is genuine, or is it a fraud?" Antony asked sitting relaxed on the couch.

"There is no way to know unless one tries it. I am not about to kill an immortal and find out." The Professor responded.

Max returned with a syringe in his hand. He walked straight towards me. I got woozy. Was he going to take my blood right here? Right now!

"Come and sit," he instructed me in a low voice.

I did not move.

"You will not feel a thing," Max said in an attempt to calm me.

My eyes glistened. "Please don't make me do this," I whispered to Dion.

He looked at me with sympathy, and then glanced at his brother. Dion placed his hand on my lower back and tried to lead me to the chair.

"When he is finished it will be like nothing ever happened," Dion said gently.

"Kasey, are you not curious to know if you are related to Pandora?" Max asked.

"I don't know. This is all so weird." Could it be possible? Am I linked to the Ancient Greeks?

My heart raced, but I sat. Max knelt on one knee beside me, grabbed my arm, and turned it outward. He pulled my sleeve up. I let out a slow breath in an attempt to calm myself. Max placed his thumb over the bend of the elbow. I trembled. His thumb began to illuminate with bright yellow rays of light. Startled, I peered at Dion. Max placed the syringe into my skin under his thumb. I felt nothing. The tube filled up with my blood. When it was half-full he removed the syringe from my skin. He placed his thumb over the tiny hole left.

He let go of my arm stood and said, "Thank you."

With my opposite hand, I ran it down my arm where the syringe had been. No trace or mark could be seen or felt. It was amazing.

Max gave the Professor a labeled vial of my blood. I proceeded to put my boots on. "Professor, do you have a copy of the curse?" Antony asked.

"Yes, here." He handed a folded paper to Antony.

"I must get back. I kept my taxi waiting. I do not want to run into your brothers," the Professor said, heading for the door.

"We knew our brothers were coming to see us. We received a vision." Martin spoke up.

"Martin saw Kasey looking at them in the club, and then I saw them headed for Deia," John said.

I remembered the two men from the club. They must have been the brothers. Dion eyed me confused.

"Why was this not told to me?" he asked aggravated.

"We did not want to ruin your evening. Had you known, would you have taken her out?" Martin asked.

Dion huffed.

"We have plenty of room here, you are welcomed to stay, old friend." Max got to the door before the Professor.

"No, no, I must go. Thank you."

"Very well then, thank you for your visit Professor. Take care, my friend," Max and the Professor shook hands.

"Give me a couple of days on the lab work," the Professor yelled on his way out.

Max closed the door. "Quite an evening we all have had," he looked at Dion.

Dion raised one eyebrow. "What does the tablet say?" he asked.

Everyone turned to Antony. He opened up the folded paper and read the curse. It was written in Greek.

"What does it say?" I whispered to Dion.

He leaned his head into me,

> "And let it be upon this immortal,
> That was sentence by mighty wraths,

> To lay eternally in the heavens,
> By the steel of his kindred's blade,
> And to thy blade's holder,
> May the Grace's gifts be now bestowed."

"Do you think the curse is true?" Martin asked.

"I do not know. It offers intriguing possibilities. We have a lot to think about." Max said somberly.

"You can't be thinking the curse is a good thing!" I blurted without thought.

"Kasey, you do not understand what our life is like. Immortality is no different from a tortured eternity. To finally be able to rest, forever, I cannot even imagine." Max snapped at me.

"I'm sorry, you're right. I don't know…But how could you allow this to happen to humanity?" I snapped right back at him.

"What does this have to do with humanity?" John asked.

"Could you imagine your brother in the mortal world with all that power? What if he's already gained some extra gifts." By the silence in the room, I could tell this was something none of them had considered.

"She is right on both counts." Dion came to my defense, thank goodness.

"She is right, Max. Even though some of us would love to end our immortality, the repercussions would come at what great cost to mortals." Martin, spoke wisely, well beyond his age of fifteen.

Max shook his head. "You all are right. We could never allow Sam to gather that much power. I pray that he has not used it yet."

"John, Martin, when should we be expecting them?" Max asked.

"We are not sure. All we got was the vision of them at the club, and then heading for Deia." John answered.

"It will be approaching dawn soon," Max said. "I believe Kasey needs to get home. We should get our rest as well." It was clear he dominated the household.

I headed for the door, and Dion followed. The others headed upstairs. When I opened the door the two men from the club stood about to knock on the door.

Dion gasped, "Sam! James!"

"Hello my good brother," Sam the older looking man said.

I could see now the similarities between the brothers. Sam had the same dark hair but slicked back with lots of gel. He wore a black suit with a black shirt. A slight goatee grew on his chin.

James appeared shaggy and casual. His hair highlighted as Dion's, except his were white tipped. He wore a black Super Mario Brothers tee shirt and had a crucifix tattooed to his arm. James followed Sam in. I heard the patter of feet coming back down the stairs. As Sam passed Dion, he gave him a judgmental nod.

"Truly disappointed," he said to Dion then looked at me. "I thought you had better sense than to get involved with a human."

"What are you doing here?" Max ordered.

"Such a harsh welcome, brother. We have not seen each other in more than a century. Where is your hospitality?"

Sam continued in, sitting himself down on the loveseat. James entered and stood next to him. The atmosphere suddenly became unnerving. The Kleon's body language and facial expressions were tight with apprehension.

"What do you want, Sam?" Dion asked.

"We happened to run into the Professor down the road. It is reasonable to assume that we do not have to explain anything. I suppose you already know."

"Did you do anything to the Professor?" Antony finally showed emotion.

"We let him be." James raised his hand in a calming way.

"Have you used the tablet's curse?" Max asked.

"No, I came to you first. What do you say brothers? Are you ready to rest in peace?" Sam asked in a condescending tone.

Max looked around the room making eye contact with his brothers. A few of them nodded.

"We appreciate the offer, but no thank you," Max said.

Sam shot up from his chair, "What! You of all people! I would have thought to have taken this offer," he raged.

"Clearly Sam, you have lost touch with who your brothers are," Max said calmly.

"Clearly," Sam looked around the room at all of them suspiciously, "Something has changed." He peered at me. "Something has interfered."

"You keep her out of this. This is between you and us." Dion stiffened his body forward and clenched his fist.

Sam walked up to Dion inches from his face. "Careful brother, remember the last time this," he glared at me, "happened to the family. Remember what it did to us. I will be back the day of the winter solstice. I hope this gives you enough time to properly think about your decision." With that, he walked out the door, James followed.

"Or what?" Dion retorted.

"We will deal with that when we must," Sam called back without turning around.

Dion slid me from out of the doorway and closed the door.

"He assumed we would let him spear us through the heart; as if it were some type of ritual," Martin said in disbelief.

"Why, though? Why does this mean so much to him? What is he after?" Antony walked back up the stairs.

"When it comes to Sam, I have stopped asking why a long time ago," John said sour.

"We will need a plan of action for when he returns. I wish to reconvene this in the morning around nine." Max said.

"I will see you at ten, Max. He is not coming for us tomorrow." Antony yawned.

Max followed his brothers upstairs

Dion opened the front door a crack and looked out. He placed his hand on my lower back and led me through the doorway. Once in his car, he sat stiff, clenching and relaxing his fingers around the steering wheel. Staring straight, he was furious. He gunned the gas of the Mini Cooper. As we reached the road from his driveway, I had to do something even though my nerves were on high alert as well.

"Yup, typical first date. Minus the Egyptologist, blood getting drawn, and slaying of immortals you are just an average Joe." I said sarcastically. That broke his intense trance and he loosened up.

"I cannot apologize to you enough. I wish I never brought you to the house tonight."

"I thought the future was inevitable. This would have happened regardless. Plus it wasn't too bad-- minus the whole blood thing. That's tripped me out." I rubbed the spot.

His expression changed to worried, "It does not hurt, does it?"

"No…no that's the trippy part. Your brother took my blood in the middle of your living room and there's no trace that it ever happened. That's freaky."

"Max has a great gift. I have watched him heal so many. I am sorry for his behavior. He can be domineering."

"What do you think about the whole Pandora thing? Can it be possible?"

"I do not know, maybe your likeness to her is simply a coincidence. We will have to wait and see what the Professor finds."

"She's an immortal, right?"

"Yes, we have never met her."

"Why can't immortals have children?" I asked.

"I do not have the answer to that technically. My theory is that God did not want the immortal gene pool to mix with humans. Can you imagine if Earth was filled with humans born to immortals and their special powers were inherited?"

"Then you wouldn't have to hide, and everyone would be like you." I crossed my arms.

He sighed, "But immortals are sterile and therefore anomalies among humans."

"Are you worried Sam might do something horrible?"

"Before we went into the cave, Sam and I were close. He was a great man. Who, like us, has paid a great price with no answers. I believe he is bitter, and it pains me to watch him lead such an unhappy eternity. If I know my brother well, if deep down somewhere he still holds true to the man I once knew, then I cannot believe he would ever kill his brothers."

"What about James?"

"James' issue is with Max. He is seventeen and does not understand what happened to him. He wants to have fun. At first, Max was terribly restricting. He demanded discipline, order, and propriety. A few centuries ago he lightened up…"

"You consider the way he behaved tonight lightened up? Whew…" I shook my head.

Dion smirked, "James is a harmless, good hearted, rebellious teenager who got in with the wrong brother."

We pulled up to the Castillo's restaurant. Dion put the car in park and turned to me. I was fascinated by our conversations on his magical world and didn't want it to end.

"It's funny I'm no longer sleepy," I said.

"Me neither. I can stay for while if you wish to converse." He leaned his head back on his headrest.

I did the same. "So tell me, Dion what kind of things do you guys do when you live forever?"

"As you can see we own some nice materialistic things. Which we feel guilty about, so to keep a balanced life we help humanity out."

"What do you mean?"

"We like to think we were given these abilities to do good in the world. So we helped out during the black plague. We go to poverty-stricken or diseased remote places around the world and assist with what we can. The longest we have ever stayed at one place was at a Franciscan Monastery during the dark ages. Other than that sometimes ten years in a region, usually it's five. We should be leaving Deia, in a year or so."

"That's amazing." I grinned.

"No...it is really not. Kasey, it does not matter how long you have lived. What you have done, or what you have seen, the world still has no rhyme or reason to it. Time and people now are as lost and muddled as they were a thousand years ago."

Dion rambled, reaching deep within his thoughts and pulling his feelings out. I relished hearing his thoughts. He seemed wise, had done so much, and gained so many experiences.

"Agh...please enough about me tonight. Let us talk about you." He turned his eyes toward me and beamed.

"Okay, fair enough. What would you like to know?" I smiled back trying to lighten up the somber mood.

"Hmmm...have you ever been to church other than here in Deia?"

I made a face at him. So much for trying to lighten up the mood.

"Yes," I said.

"Really!" He was suprised.

"As a matter of fact, I'm baptized Catholic." I gave him an, ah-ha look.

Shocked he said, "No! Please do explain."

"Well, the last time I set foot in a church was the day I was baptized. Apparently, my grandfather was persistent that I get baptized. According to my father, my grandfather took me down one day and did it. They say he was a fanatic about angels and saints." I gave him an impish look. "I bet he'd be thrilled if he knew I was dating one now."

"Interesting," he caressed my cheek with his knuckles. With soft eyes, he looked at me lovingly.

"Which part?" I asked.

"The fact that you were baptized, of course."

"Oh."

He smirked, "After all, with John around, I already knew we would be dating."

I scoffed. He was so cocky at times. I removed his hand from my cheek and tossed it in his lap. He laughed. I yawned unwillingly.

"I think you are getting sleepy, Kasey."

"I think I am too."

He opened his car door and then opened mine. Madhu's words repeated in my head: "You will know by the kiss."

I didn't allow him to kiss me earlier. Would he try again? Feeling sick with the unknown, I wasn't sure I was ready to feel another man's lips on mine. We walked hand in hand up to the restaurant door. The rosy pink hue of the day's light skimmed the horizon. The key hole was hard to see. As I fumbled with the keys, there was a click from the lock inside, and the door opened. On the other side, Beatriz stood in her robe.

Startled, I squeaked, "Morning Sra. Beatriz."

"*Buenos Dias*, Kasey…Dion." She turned and walked back into the restaurant.

I hoped he didn't notice my embarrassed red my cheeks. Dion chuckled, leaned over, and kissed my forehead.

"Sleep well Kasey, sweet dreams."

"Thanks, you as well." Relieved he hadn't tried a real kiss, I turned and entered the restaurant.

## 11. Kasey and Hercules

Dion and I spent the next two weeks casually dating. We saw each other every other afternoon. He backed off some after our bizarre first date. He didn't try to kiss me again. Could he be waiting for me to make the first move?

His answers to my questions were always fascinating. I became familiar with how his world worked, and the awkwardness of it didn't bothered me. Instead, I became engrossed in his magical supernatural world.

Madhu and Bernardo lasted a week; he wanted someone who would go the distance. It didn't faze her, she had already moved on to someone else at the local bakery. I spoke with Nolan once a week. It went well for him in his new living arrangements and my parents are my parents.

Tonight I was going to Dion's opening night at the theater. The anticipation of seeing him on stage prevented me from focusing on my term paper. A knock on the door came as a welcomed distraction.

"*Entra*," I yelled out.

*Señor* Castillo opened my door and walked in. I stood.

"Kasey, *un momento*, do you have a minute?" he asked. He held an old cigar box.

I gestured for him to sit on the desk chair while I sat on the bed.

"Kasey, I was hoping I could speak to you about something personal." He stumbled with his words and looked quite uncomfortable. His hand rubbed the back of his neck as he stretched it out.

I became apprehensive myself, "its okay *senor*."

He let out a deep breath, "Kasey, I know I am not your father, but you are staying here under our care, and I feel …I feel I should at least give you my advice."

Oh no, he's going to talk to me about Dion.

"I know you have started relations with Dion Kleon and even though they are a nice good family…" He paused. "Please be careful for yourself. They…well they are a different kind of family and I wish you to be cautious. Try not to get yourself involved with them too much." His eyebrows furrowed.

Did he know their secret? It sounded like he was warning me against what they are.

"Here, in this box, are some old pictures of my family and our restaurant here in Deia. It shows how time has not affected the village. Take a close look at the first one. If you wish, we can speak again." He left the cigar box on the chair and walked out.

I opened the box and saw a pile of black and white photos inside. I picked up the first picture. A man and his young son of eight or nine were standing in front of the *El Caracoles* restaurant. The restaurant looked different, but not too much. I flipped the photo over and the writing on the back read 1938, *Alejandro y Rodrigo Castillo*. I'd seen other photos of the Castillo family and knew that Alejandro was Fernando's father and Rodrigo was Fernando's grandfather. Turning over the photo, I examined it further. That's when I saw it. In the background, five men sat at a table. Their faces were like haunting ghosts. The Kleon brothers, dressed in outfits from the early twentieth century, looked preserved in time.

A chill ran through my body. The reality of Dion's immortality hit me like a stone hitting a serene pond. I knew he was immortal, but the visual left me sick and confused. Not sure what emotions I should be feeling, I put the picture back in the cigar box and closed it. What did I get myself into?

The phone rang at that moment. Dion was calling, and it was probably not a coincidence.

"Hi." I attempted to sound normal.

"Hello, is everything all right?"

"Yes, why would you ask? You don't have Martin and John spying on me, do you?"

"Well... are you sure everything is all right?"

"I'm fine. Are you ready for the performance?" I tried to redirect our conversation.

"Okay... yes. I am ready. Quite nervous."

"Why? Haven't you done this for thousands of years?"

"Um ...yes and normally I would not be this nervous. But your presence in the audience has me anxious."

"Would you rather I not come?" I asked coldly.

"Well no, I want you to go. Are you sure nothing is bothering you?"

"I'm fine. I'll be there," I snapped.

"With Sam and James still hanging around the island it would put my mind at ease, if you rode with my brothers."

"That's fine then. See you later."

"Bye Kasey." He hesitated before he hung up.

I ate my seafood medley soup around eight and decided to wait downstairs for his brothers to come pick me up. Fernando avoided eye contact the whole evening. The black Mercedes van pulled up, and I walked out to it. Antony was in the driver's seat. John, Martin, and Max sat in the back seats. Martin opened the sliding door, hopped out and opened the front door for me.

"*Buenas noches* Kasey."

"*Buenas noches*," I replied in kind. I wasn't sure how to feel about a whole car ride with Dion's brothers minus Dion. It was unnerving. I had never hung out with any of them, just Dion. As we got going, the awkward silence in the car got to me, so I broke it.

"I'm sure you guys have seen Dion do this a million times. Is he good?"

"Very," Antony answered.

"What was his best role?" I asked.

"Phantom," Martin, John, and Antony said simultaneously.

"He was the phantom in Phantom of the Opera?"

"He has done that one a couple of times, but that first time he performed it, was the best performance I have ever seen him do," Martin answered.

"He also did a stellar job with Laertes, back in the day." Antony chimed in.

"Hamlet's Laertes?" I asked.

"Yes, under the direction of Shakespeare in the Rose Theater. That was memorable to watch," Antony elaborated.

My jaw dropped. "Seriously?" I asked, dumbfounded.

John chuckled. "Seriously Kase, we have met some pretty significant people through time."

"Most of the time, we had no idea they were going to be these world icons," Antony said.

"Who has been the most memorable person you have met?"

"That's a loaded question," John said.

"I would say Joan," Martin said without a hesitation.

"Joan who?"

"Joan of Arc," Antony answered.

I turned and looked at Martin. "What was she like?"

"Amazing. The will-power she had for her cause made even the immortals feel inconsequential."

Before now, I'd never seen Martin demonstrate such passion for anything. I could hear longing in his voice.

"Martin crushed on her," John teased.

I smiled at Martin. He turned and looked out the window bothered.

"I'm sorry. Was she close to you guys?" I didn't know much about her. Only that she burned at the stake.

"No, we met her a few times. She was a busy girl. She would not even look twice at Martin," John said.

"It was her God given destiny to lead the French army against the English. She was given a great purpose in this life to fulfill and she accepted it nobly," Martin honored her with his words.

Since Dion and I started dating, Max avoided me. He never came by the restaurant anymore. No one said anything, but by the way he treated me I could tell he was not fond of the fact that I was dating Dion. I couldn't help wonder if it was because I was human or not religious.

We pulled into the packed dirt parking lot. The theater was unique and something I'd never seen. It was an open-air theater on the side of a mountain. The stadium style stoned seating sloped downward to a state of the art stage. Complete with orchestra pit, sidewalls, and ornate curtains. It was a perfect blend of a sixth century Greek theater with modern day characteristics.

Max led the way to our center stage seats, but John stopped me from sitting.

"Would you like to see Dion back stage before the show?" he asked.

"No, I'm okay. I'll see him after," I replied.

"Um…well he wants to see you. Come on." He grabbed my hand and pulled me along.

"Did you have a vision?" His actions confused me.

"Nope, he told me he wanted to see you before the show. I was to make sure I brought you by."

We walked behind the stage walls, and like any typical theater the manic and mayhem that goes on before a show was at full blast. Despite the hectic atmosphere, John took me right to the actor's area. All the actors were in costumes, huddled together, down on their knees deep in prayer. I felt strange watching them pray, as if I walked in on a private moment. John left me there and returned to his seat. When the group finished, they made the sign of the cross and stood. Dion came to me at once.

"*Hola*, I am glad you came." He gleamed.

"Me too," I answered giving him a hug. His skin felt warm. I felt guilty for being cross with him earlier. I couldn't imagine how he wasn't cold in his short roman toga. Then again, did he even get cold?

"Really?" He questioned, "You seemed upset earlier. Was something bothering you?"

"Yes, but I'm okay. I don't want you to worry about me. I want you to worry about your performance."

"Why would I worry? I have this down."

I scoffed, "You're a Saint. Aren't you supposed to have humility?"

"Yeah, I am bad about that one from time to time." He shrugged his shoulders. "You know, you can always come to me with anything that is bothering you." He lifted my chin with his closed fist forcing me to look at him.

"I know…I know…" I removed my chin from his hand.

"We are going to start soon. You should probably get back to your seat. Thank you again."

"It's my pleasure. Break a leg."

He grinned at my comment. We kissed on the cheek and parted. I went back and took my place between John and Antony. As the orchestra started the overture, I looked around at the audience, amazed at how many people filled in since we arrived. I gazed to my right and my heart stopped.

I must have stiffen in my seat because Antony leaned over and asked, "Kasey, what is wrong?"

"Sam and James are sitting over there." I motioned my head in their direction. Antony looked, and then, without saying a word, he caught the eyes of John, Max, and Martin to let them know. They nodded when they saw what we had.

The lights on the stage dimmed, and the play began. Dion was incredible. A true actor. I forgot Dion played a role and accepted him as Hercules in Spanish. The orchestra, cast, and crew all did such a phenomenal job. The audience gave a standing ovation. As soon as the curtain came down, the bright lights on stage were back, Max huddled close to us.

"Let us go back stage I want to avoid Sam and James."

We did what he commanded and made a beeline for the back stage. The celebrations were loud and chaotic. I followed the Kleon brothers putting my faith in them that they would lead me to Dion. Max spotted him first. He was by the dressing stations receiving congratulations.

"Job well done, brother," Max said grabbing Dion's shoulder and shaking his hand.

"You were amazing." I hugged and gave him a pop kiss on the mouth without any thought to it, but it caught him off guard. His other brothers congratulated him, too.

"Thank you let me go change out of the costume. Give me about ten minutes."

We waited for him to return. When he came back Max said, "We should get out of here. See you back home."

"Thank you, thanks a million," Dion smiled and said his farewells to his brothers.

"Kasey, you shall ride back with me." He led me through all the chaos and celebrations stopping at brief times to say congratulations or to receive congratulations from fellow cast mates.

As soon as we approached the car, we heard someone screaming Dion's name. We turned to see John sprinting toward us, his face troubled. When he reached us, he pulled Dion away and spoke to him in private. Then Dion looked anxious he nodded and John left. Dion came back to the car looking stone serious.

In the car I asked, "What's wrong?"

"Nothing," he said, frigid.

I began to buckle myself in and his hand stopped mine. "Do not buckle."

"What! Why not?"

"Kasey please…"

"Dion, did John and Martin see something?" I asked alarmed but returning my seatbelt back in place. He began to open the roof to the convertible.

"Isn't it chilly tonight to ride with the roof down?" I was annoyed at his strange behavior.

"Kasey, trust me, please," he placed his hand on my leg and gave me a nervous smile.

"Errr, you drive me nuts," I turned my head toward the road.

"So, how did you like the play?" he asked changing the subject.

"It was great. You're talented." I grumbled. I developed a nasty chill from the cold wind that blew at us. I shivered several times in my seat. He looked at me apologetically, "Thank you, you really thought so."

"Of course I did. You certainly have a gift. Have you ever tried Hollywood?"

"Naturally, in the forties and fifties, but it was not for me. I prefer the theater feel with a live audience."

"You mention the forties and fifties like they were yesterday." His nonchalant manner toward time amused me.

"When you live as long as I have the forties and fifties seem like they were yest…"

He jerked the wheel violently swerving the car. My screams bellowed through the open car. A huge boulder fell from nowhere and landed directly in front of us. With Dion's quick reflexes, he veered the car, screeching the tires around the boulder. Once we were driving straight again, I braced myself with the side of the door. Tiny pebbles hit the windshield, imitating a downpour. In a matter of minutes, the glass shattered into a million pieces.

Dion grabbed the back of my neck and pushed my head down toward my lap. I covered myself with my arms as I felt the glass fall upon me. When he let go, I dusted off the glass pieces and sat upright in my seat. I looked out through the glassless windshield in time to see a giant tree flying toward us. He swerved the car attempting to miss the tree, but the tree seemed to be mimicking the car's every move. If he jerked right, the tree swiftly glided through the air to its right. If he jerked left, the tree followed in the same pattern. It finally landed a few feet from the car. An impact was inevitable.

Dion let go of the steering wheel and jumped over me. He picked me up and pressed me close. The pressure felt like I hit a stonewall. He held me tight against him and evacuated our bodies from the moving vehicle.

We rolled through the air, and his back hit the pavement hard. At speeds, I cannot imagine, he skidded on his back holding me close to his chest. He roared in pain. I held on tight to his shirt, but as we were slowing, my lower body slipped off him and my hip skidded on the pavement. I felt a low stinging sensation. When we stopped, he rolled me off and grunted in pain. His shirt shredded. There was a brief second of pain in his face then he popped up on one knee, as if the road hadn't ripped off his skin. His flesh healed rapidly. Any injuries were disappearing.

"Kasey, are you hurt?" Dion drew my attention to him. My heart pounded with every heavy breath I took. The impact knocked the wind out of my lungs. I wanted to reply but couldn't.

"Kasey, say something, can you move. What hurts?" He placed one hand behind my ear and the other on my rib cage. He looked panicked.

"Kasey, look at me. Are you hurt?"

I shook my head no. I pointed at what I was seeing. The front of the car hit the tree at such speed that the car flipped foreword. Beyond the tree, James ran disappearing into the forest. I whispered, "James."

"Stay here. Do not move. Let Max look at you." He took a quick look up and down my body. Once he was content I wasn't hurt, he was gone.

Seconds later, a black Mercedes pulled up with great urgency, and his brothers ran out. Max reached me first. The others followed Dion.

"Kasey, hold still." Max said. His hand began to glow, and he scanned my body as Dion had with his eyes.

I sat up and pulled my shirt over my hip concealing my torn clothing, "I'm fine." I managed to say.

Max's eyebrows wrinkled. "Kasey, are you sure?"

"I'm okay, really. I'm not hurt." I ignored the stinging coming from my right hip. Max placed his hand on my shoulder.

"Kasey, if you are injured I can help." He was troubled. Did he know?

"I'm okay. I don't need your help." The tears began to stream down my face, even though I didn't want to cry. I tried to wipe them away. At that moment, the Kleon brothers came back huffing big breaths of cold air. Dion came straight towards me and helped me up. We hugged. I buried my face into his cold, frayed shirt. Underneath the slashed shirt, his skin was warm and comforting.

"What happened?" Antony asked.

"The tree flew toward us. It landed right in front of the car."

I trembled, "So, I did see that right! How?" My voice hoarse from all the screaming I did.

"James' telekinesis. He moved the tree with his mind," Max said.

"Why?" I asked.

"I am not sure," Max answered.

"Man, I really liked this car too," John said. He and Martin examined the wreckage.

"Did you find them?" Max asked upset.

"No, I could not even pick up a trace." Dion's muscles tensed under my arms.

"Wait we have something!" Martin and John said simultaneously. Their eyes were the most disturbing eyes I had ever seen. Their dark eyeballs disappeared into their eyelids, and all that remained was the glossy white. They looked like they were some form of human aliens.

"I see Sam and James fleeing. They are not on main roads," Martin said bringing his eyes back to their normal state.

"I see them in Soller. They will check into a hotel room." John looked like himself again.

"I doubt they will remain there all night," Max said.

"Should we go after them? Soller is not far," Dion asked.

"No, I do not think they will be back, but we should stay on high alert throughout the night. John, Martin anymore visions let us know," Max's authoritative nature felt comforting.

"Of course," they answered.

"Come. Let us go," Antony suggested. "We will call the authorities and inform them of your accident. They can clear the road."

Everyone headed back toward the black Mercedes.

"Dion, I want to go home." I desired the safe walls of my small cubby of a room.

"Of course, we will stop there first. Can I come with you or do you wish to be alone?"

"You can come. That's fine."

He kept his arm around me the entire car ride. The mood in the car was somber. I tried to hold my composure in front of his brothers.

They dropped us off at the restaurant. Antony let Dion wear his shirt. Fernando and Beatriz were busy with customers. Catalina helped in the kitchen. We snuck by everyone and went upstairs. He closed the door behind me, and I let out a big sigh of relief. Then I shook uncontrollably and wept. I brought my hands to my face. Dion wrapped his arms around my back and held me close.

"I am so sorry," I said ashamed.

"Why are you apologizing to me? I am the one who is sorry you experienced something terrifying tonight." He leaned his chin on top of my head. I backed up from him taking small quick breaths.

"I'll be alright." I wiped my face and attempted a smile. "Could I get you something?"

"No I am perfectly fine, thank you," he said.

"Well, I need to use the restroom, and I think I'm going to change into something more comfortable. I'm not planning on going anywhere else tonight."

I rummaged through my drawer and pulled out my black loose lounge shorts with my wonder woman t-shirt. He sat on my bed with his back leaning up against the wall. I closed the door to the bathroom and lowered my plaid green pants down to my thighs. The scrape on my hip bled onto my underwear. The wound was the size of my hand. I cleaned it with some peroxide and cringed every time I patted it. I found some big gauze in the bathroom and, I covered the scrape. I welcomed my loose shorts. After too much time in the bathroom, I finally came out.

Dion sat on the bed with Fernando's cigar box in his lap. He rummaged through the pictures.

His eyes narrowed at me. "When did you get these?"

"Just before the play this afternoon." I put my cloths away and sat next to him.

"Ah, that explains why you were acting strange. Who gave you these pictures?"

"Fernando."

"Did he say anything when he gave them to you?"

"He wanted to warn me to be careful and to not get too close to you and your brothers."

"Interesting. What bothered you about this?" He grabbed my hand and started to rub the inside of my palm with his thumb.

"I know what you are, but when I was given that photo taken so long ago with you in it, it really bothered me."

"I wonder if I am being selfish in allowing our attraction to go on. I mean, I could try to cheat fate and keep running from it. I am fast," he smirked.

"Does that work?"

"No." He raised the back of my hand to his lips and kissed it. "We will figure it out somehow. We will make it work for us. No matter what we have to do."

"Have you heard back from the Professor?" I asked.

"No."

"I would really like to know if I'm related to an immortal."

"Why. We are not that great."

I crossed my arms. "Let's say that I am. I could be sitting here with some kind of special ability and wouldn't even know it."

"Ah, you want super powers, do you?"

"Of course."

"Maybe, I can help figure out if you have one. Is there anything you can think of, that happens to you sometimes, that doesn't feel natural or human?"

"Actually yes, my stomach cramps just before something serious, dangerous, or bad is to happen. I thought those feeling were some type of sixth sense."

"Well, there you have it. That could be your super power." He scooted closer to me.

"What! That's lame."

He laughed. "No one said it had to be extravagant."

"Figures, I wouldn't get a cool power." I sulked.

"Kasey, that's probably not even a power. Let us hope you are not related to Pandora. You do not want any part of this world."

"Why?"

"After what happened tonight you really have to ask?" His whole body tensed once he brought up the accident.

"Do you think your brothers are going to try to kill us again?"

"I don't die, and I doubt they were trying to kill you."

"How can you say that? James threw a tree at your car with me in it!"

"True, but he knew you were with me. I would never let anything happen to you."

With his other hand, he pulled my hair away from my cheek. My heart thumped with the anticipation that he might kiss me. I leaned forward a tad but cringed from the pain on my hip.

"Kasey… I wish to discuss something… but I do not want you to feel like I am prying into your personal matters," he said apprehensive.

I wasn't sure to what he was leading into. "Whatever it is you can say it."

"I know you received an abrasion on your hip from the accident tonight."

His comment disturbed me.

"Max told me before we entered the restaurant. Why did you not let us know you were injured?" he asked.

I huffed. "I really have no privacy with your brothers around do I?"

"Some, but not really."

"How did he figure it out?" I asked.

"Max has a great gift. He is like a human diagnostic machine. He can scan a body, know what is wrong, and then proceed to fix the broken parts."

"Does he have any limits?"

"Yes, he cannot cure disease. He can mend flesh, bones, muscles, and purge all pain. When he scanned you at the site, he realized you hurt your hip, but you insisted that you were fine. He respected your wishes and did not pursue it any further. Why did you not let us know you were hurt? He could have taken care of your wound and you would not have any pain right now," Dion asked concerned.

My cheeks blushed. "It's not that bad, and I was uncomfortable with the idea…" I glanced down embarrassed.

"Kasey, he is a doctor, and quite possibly the best doctor in the world. I hate the thought of you sitting here cringing in pain when he could have taken care of it."

"Pain is part of life." I smirked, "In a few days it will start to heal."

"If you change your mind, tomorrow he can make it disappear."

I nodded. "Thanks."

"One other topic of conversation I wish to address," he said.

"Boy, you sure are on a roll tonight. What?"

He leaned in close to my face. "You kissed me after the play."

My stomach descended like the plunge feeling when the airplane drops. "It was just a peck of congratulations, that's all."

His breath felt warm on my lips. "Would you mind if I continued the celebration here, now?" he whispered.

Goosebumps filled my whole body. "No, I don't mind," I whispered back. I closed my eyes and let the sense of his soft smooth, lips glide across mine. I tried to lean into him, but the movement upset my hip, and I winced in pain.

He backed off. "I know I am rusty, but was it that painful?"

I laughed at his comment. He played with my hair and moved it back.

"You silly girl." With a gentle touch, he placed his hand above my right hip and guided my body so that I was lying on my left side. He started to kiss me. His lips barely touched mine. Did he think I was made of breakable glass? The thought made me chuckle.

He backed up and cocked his head to the side. "Is this amusing?"

Horrified that my thoughts got the better of me, I blushed. "No…no…not at all." I gazed at his shirt avoiding his eyes.

"Is everything alright? I was not kidding on the rusty part."

Poor thing he was so confused. Here we were, embraced in a passionate kiss, and I giggled.

"No...I mean yes, yes, everything is perfect," I tried to compose myself.

He eyed me uncertain and I looked back at him. He took his hand and precisely weaved his fingers into my hair. He barely held the back of my neck. I swallowed, nervous. This time there was nothing gentle about his kiss. His lips were full of strength and authority. He was full of passion. Entirely consumed with desire, he cleansed all traces of the giggles away.

## 12. Dion's Innocence

Kasey is my serendipity, angelic, and surreal asleep in her tiny twin bed. Cuddled into her pillow, she is everything happiness claims to be. I watched her squirm as the rays from the outside sunlight beamed down on her pastel face. She fluttered her eyes. Like a bloomed bouquet of gardenias, her smile gave purpose to my existence.

"Good morning," I said first.

"Good morning, did you stay up in that chair all night?"

"No, I took a pillow and slept on the floor." I picked up the pillow lying next to her bed.

She shook her head. "That was silly you could have…"

"I am a gentleman, I would not unless invited." I sat beside her and ran my fingers down her arm. Leaning in for a good morning bliss, I pecked her. Our lips touched, barely brushing against each other. Applying more pressure, we kissed. Each moment of my one thousand, seven hundred, and sixty-one years of life was worth every kiss, every touch, and every look she gave me. With just a smile, a thousand years of time, forgotten.

She broke first, "Mmm…Good morning." She smiled.

"I should be going before the house stirs. If I leave now I can speed out of here without anyone ever knowing."

"All right, I'll see you this afternoon after school." She caressed my hand with hers.

"I will be at the theater for most of the evening. Would you come and visit back stage until I am through?"

"Sure, sounds like a plan."

We kissed goodbye. Then I sped out of her room and out of the restaurant at half my capable speed.

I arrived home with some fresh baked goods for breakfast. The house started to stir with the aroma of food and coffee. The first ones down to the kitchen were John and Martin.

"Sweet, breakfast," they said.

Antony and Max were not far behind. Max took one look at my clothing and shook his head. John laughed. We sat at the squared kitchen table to eat.

"Was there any other signs of them last night?" Antony asked.

"No, they did not come around to her place," I replied.

"They are not dim-witted. I do not think they will be back for another few days." Max ate a cheese pastry.

"So help them if they come again and try to harm her... I am ready to use that spell myself." My fingers tightened around the coffee mug handle. Max stood up, grabbed my shirt, and pulled me up.

"This is exactly what it does to a man," he snarled. His eyes maddened with rage. "Do not lose yourself to revenge and anger because you love her. If you are going to take this relationship on Dion, you cannot lose track of the man you are."

It has been decades since Max demonstrated this type of anger. He pushed me back into my chair, sat down, and placed his hand over his eyes. John and Martin sat frozen, jaws dropped.

Antony took another bite of his strawberry strudel. "Max, Dion is not Sam," he said with his mouth full.

Max looked up with regret surrounding his eyes.

"I know exactly what love does to a man." I gripped Max's shoulder with a strong hold, "I have watched it happen to two of the finest men I know. I am aware of whom I am, and I will never lose sight of that. And you, as well as anyone here know love is not something we choose, it chooses us." I could not swallow the lump stuck in my throat, "when it is over, and she has passed, I am going to need you brother," to my surprise, the words came out.

Stone serious, Max replied, "I will be there." He took hold of my shoulder and shook it as a promise. Then he grabbed his pastry and went upstairs. I exhaled with relief.

"You know this whole thing with you and Kasey is hard for him," Antony said, "It has brought back memories and emotions of Cyra that he has not dealt with for centuries."

"To be honest, I am terrified to end up like him or Sam. Our lives now have little to no meaning or purpose, but without her, it would have none."

"Max isn't the only one that will be here for you. We will carry you through the years for all eternity," John said with a sympathetic grin.

"With any luck there will be an end to us all someday." With a solemn gaze Martin stood and left.

******

Three days since the accident there was still, no word or sign of Sam or James in Deia.

I prepared to go to the restaurant for lunch, when Kassandra, from the Spanish novella, my ringtone for Kasey, bellowed in my pocket.

"Hello beautiful." I said.

"You need to get to the restaurant right now!" she shrieked. I took off towards her at high speed. I made it there before she could speak her next words. I found her standing in front of the restaurant with phone in hand.

"What is it? What is wrong?" My hands grabbed hold of her waist.

Surprised that I appeared so quickly, she said, "Um…I'll have to remember to use those words with caution. Next time." Kasey hung the phone up. She looked grave.

"James is inside having lunch with Catalina," she whispered.

"What?" I took a step to the side and peered into the restaurant. At a far corner table Catalina and my brother James sat, laughing, and chatting.

"Uh, what is he up too?" I asked.

"I don't know. You could imagine my surprise."

"Well, let us go in for some lunch and see what he does," I suggested.

"Do you think he will do something in public?"

"No, I do not, but maybe he will leave."

We walked into the restaurant, and I took a seat at a table near the front. James saw me, and our eyes met with stern looks. Catalina turned to see Kasey and me. She scoffed and spun back to James. She made a comment, and he smiled at her. I sat at a table.

Kasey did not sit.

"Do you think he's told her that he's your brother?" She asked bothered by the situation.

"I do not know."

"Here, tell me what you want, and I will start preparing it in the back."

"Could you bring me the chorizo sandwich, please?"

Kasey headed toward the kitchen. I took short side-glances at James and Catalina. They were smitten with each other. As Kasey approached with my lunch, it seemed that they finished theirs. They stood, James hung his arm around Catalina's shoulder, and they proceeded to walk towards the exit. As they passed our table James, smiled at us, leaned in, and kissed her lips.

Appalled Kasey sat. "We have got to do something! She has no idea who he is!"

"I cannot imagine what he is up to with Catalina." I was dumbfounded. "Let me eat. Then I think I know where those two would hide out away from the world."

Kasey ate a small salad. She never ate too much in one sitting. She pecked at her food like a bird. When we finished, I realized I ran here and was without my new rented convertible.

"Kasey, give me a minute. Let me go home and bring my car."

She looked at me oddly. "Why? We can take mine."

Gently I asked, "Can I drive?"

She glared as if she was going to pick me up and throw me across the street.

"I do not mean to offend, but you are not safe behind the wheel on the Spanish roads. You might be a great driver back in America, but here you simply terrify me."

"Well it's not the easiest thing to get used to driving here. It's different from America. What are you worried about anyways? It's not like you can die if I wreck." She dangled the keys, insinuating I follow her.

Once we got in the car she asked, "Where to?"

"The ancient ruins."

The trip only took ten minutes. The forest path that led to the stones would have taken a normal human twenty minutes. I did not want to waste time. I scooped her up and sped through the forest. The shady woods were peaceful and serene with only the sounds of chirping birds. As we approached, I stopped and placed Kasey down, in case they were there. The clearing consisted of, broken pieces of huge rocks scattered everywhere.

I motioned to Kasey to be silent. We crept behind a big stone wall and peered out to see if James and Catalina were amidst the ruins. They sat close on a flat slate, embracing each other, and sharing deep, zealous kisses. I nodded in their direction, and Kasey acknowledged she spotted them as well.

I picked up a small pebble and then threw it into the middle of the ruins. James stood up and looked in our direction. I grabbed Kasey's hand, and we made ourselves known. With light footsteps, we walked around the stone.

Catalina stood angry. "What do you think you are doing here? Are you spying on me?"

James was furious. He hunched down, grunted like a bull, and challenged me to charge with his fist closed. I let go of Kasey's hand, closed my fist, and ran towards my younger brother. He reciprocated my charge. We collided. I landed a fist right into his temple, knocking him to the ground. He groaned. He kicked into my knee and shoved my legs out from under me. His thrust sent me to the ground on my back. He popped up and landed his fist right into my chest. I grunted at the hard impact. Then I grabbed his neck and hurled him over onto his back. I did not care who was watching I was going to let my little brother have it after what he did to us. Catalina screamed.

"Stop it. What is wrong with you, Dion?"

Kasey put her arm across my chest.

"Stop," she said in a soft voice.

Catalina went over to James and helped him up. He fumed.

"Catalina. Please. We came to warn you about him," Kasey began.

"Against James, Dion charged him!" Catalina screamed.

"He is my brother and there is bad blood between us." I dusted my pants off.

Catalina's eyes went wide. "You are his brother?"

"Yes, although we have not spoken for many years," James answered.

"Catalina, you don't know who he is. He can't be trusted." Kasey broke in.

"He is a master magician, Catalina. An illusionist. Do not trust what you see. I bet he has shown you things." I warned her. I was sure James used his telekinesis to lure her. For a moment, she looked at him with doubt, but then got irritated.

"Look, Catalina, I know you don't like me for whatever bizarre reasons, but I'm trying to protect you," Kasey pleaded again. Catalina narrowed her eyes at Kasey.

"Listen to Kasey. She is a good person." I persisted.

Catalina rolled her eyes and scoffed, "She is one of them. She cannot be trusted."

"She is nothing like the American who dated your sister. You have to let go of that ignorant notion of yours." I said.

"He killed her because of his recklessness. They are all thoughtless and care only about themselves." Her cheeks reddened.

"Catalina, the American did not kill your sister. Elena was driving the car that night. Both drank too much and Elena drove off the road."

"*Mentiroso*, you liar!" Catalina screamed at me.

"I am not lying. The authorities did not have the heart to tell your parents the truth. This town loves your family. They blamed the American and covered up the truth. Go ask them. Find out for yourself," I pressed.

She lost her composure and the tears fell. She shook her head.

"I do not believe you," she whispered. James put his arm around her.

"Catalina, please, you don't know what you are getting yourself into with him. You want to stay away from him, believe me. We are telling you the truth." Kasey warned her. Did she caution Catalina from dating James because he was reckless or because of what we were? Did Kasey feel the same way?

Catalina became furious. "Oh, like you are honest. Ask her, Dion, about the love letters she gets every month from her fiancé. He cannot wait for her to come home."

"How dare you go through my desk!" Kasey snapped.

"I am sure Dion has not been totally honest either. I bet he has not mentioned his ex-wife." James said.

Catalina's eyes grew wide. "Dion has an ex-wife!" She whispered to James.

"Come. let us get out of here." James pulled Catalina along and they disappeared down the path.

Kasey and I stood still and silent for several minutes.

"Well, that surely backfired." I took a seat on one of the stones.

Kasey nodded and sat herself across from me.

"So…" she said after a while.

Curious about the fiancé, I fished first, "For once, allow me to ask the questions."

"Okay, that's fair." She looked nervous.

"Is he the man Martin saw in his vision?" I asked.

"Yes, his name is Teal Bentley." She avoided my eyes.

"Is he your fiancé?"

She glanced away toward the path. I bet she wished she could escape.

"He was," she said.

"Please, do elaborate." Why would she keep this from me?

"We met our freshman year of high school. We started dating when I was a sophomore and he was a junior. He graduated this past May. I thought I was in love with him. He was perfect for me in every way."

I shifted with annoyance. I did not want to hear this, but I knew I must.

She continued. "He's natural and has a great love for the beach. He's even vegetarian sympathetic. He gets along with my parents and my brother. In fact, my brother is living with him as we speak." She looked away and began to play with her fingers. "Since he was raised in a foster home, when he turned eighteen, they set him up with his own place. Between him having no parents, and me having uninvolved parents we were a perfect self-sufficient couple." She stood and began to pace.

"Everything was perfect. This past February he asked me to marry him. Of course, I said yes. My life was following a precise plan. We agreed to marry after my graduation. Something bothered me. It was too perfect. It was like there was a missing piece. I became confused. I didn't know what to think. I distanced myself from him. Teal noticed my change and that's when we argued all the time. Then in the spring, I left him." She ran her hand through her hair roughly. Did she love him still?

"Angered and hurt, the break was hard on both of us. Just because I couldn't commit doesn't mean I don't care for him. We went through so much together, he taught me how to drive, both our proms, he was my firs…" she rambled, not thinking about her words.

I raised my eyebrows at what she almost said. Would she elaborate on the topic? The subject struck my curiosity.

She kept going ignoring the topic. "After we broke up he got angry and did something stupid out of spite. He hooked up with the first beach hussy that threw herself at him that same week. I signed up to study abroad in Spain two weeks later. He tried to mend our relationship before my trip. I avoided him. He loves me, and I thought we were in love. After coming here I've realize it isn't love, just companionship."

I understood and gave her a smile. She looked away.

"He didn't want me to come to Spain. He's called a couple of times and sent those letters, but I haven't replied," she sighed and lowered her eyes to the ground.

"I am sorry. It seems like it has been difficult." I sympathized.

"It has, I feel awful for hurting him." She looked up. "Alright, now you know about my ex-fiancé. Why don't you tell me about your ex-wife?" She raised one eyebrow in a questioning manner.

I glared down. "It is not what you think. When we awoke from the cave, we were celebrities, highly thought of in the city. A lord offered Max his daughter's hand in marriage. Back then that was a great honor. He took her. Cyra was great. Then Max, being head of the manor, chose a wife for Sam. Sholeh and Sam adored each other. Finally, he decided I needed to be married. He chose a mercantile's daughter, Lilac. She and I did what was expected of us, but we were anything but compatible. It was a dry, lifeless marriage"

Kasey sat emotionless. I wanted something from her to gauge her thoughts. "We kept our powers a secret, but after we realized we were not aging, we had to tell our wives. We needed to move from the city. Cyra and Sholeh would have followed their husbands to the ends of the Earth. They loved each other and accepted us for who we were. Lilac did not. She felt this was some type of curse and wanted nothing to do with me. I settled her with her family and assured they sought after her until her death, I left and never saw her again."

"Huh, not what I expected," Kasey said, perplexed.

"Told you it is not what you think."

"Why didn't Antony get a wife?"

"He was not around. At first when we discovered we had abilities, Antony took off. He left to figure himself out. Antony needs breaks from humanity at times. He will sometimes disappear and live completely in the wild with his animal friends. He never really wanted to par take in societal norms."

Kasey shook her head in understanding.

"I have a question," I said and wondered how she was going to take my inquiry. "Earlier you mentioned that Teal was your first."

She looked away pacing in place.

"Geez, Dion. Do we have to talk about this?" Her demeanor changed. She became jittery.

"I would like to, but if you wish not to…"

She turned bright red, "It's a different world over there. I don't want you to think…"

"Kasey, stop worrying about what I think, I want to know you, as you are, and who you are." I could not fathom why she worried so much. How much of herself did she hide from me? It was preposterous. How could she think she was anything but wonderful the way she is?

"I'm not going to stop worrying. You're a freaking Saint, Dion. That's hard to live up to. You guys are these icons who have done extraordinary things and lived extraordinary lives. I don't even come close to those values. I'm from the other side of the tracks. Personally, my virginity never bothered me until I met you…" She was in a panic.

I went to her, "Kasey," I held her chin up. "Remember even the saints were human, and therefore, not flawless."

She calmed down. I rubbed her shoulders and arms.

"Simply because I am ancient does not mean I am clueless as to the current times we live in. I was not sure but I assumed you were not a virgin."

She backed off from me offended. "Why?"

"You had a few things going against you. You are an American eighteen year old, without religion, and with hippie parents."

"What? That's messed up Dion."

I raised one eyebrow at her.

"Okay, fine. Teal was my first and only. He and I practically lived together before we broke up," she said.

The conversation caused her anxiety. I would be lying to myself if I said I was not disappointed that she was not mine to have first. I could not hold the actions of her past against her. That would not be fair. She is her own beautiful person and God sent me this angel with all her perfections and imperfections.

"What about you Dion. A thousand years?"

Was she hoping that I was sexually promiscuous? Did she think that would make her feel less guilty?

"I was married before." I smiled at her.

She huffed. "Is that it?"

"Yes, I would never without being married to a girl first." I was honest.

She rolled her eyes.

I laughed, reached out, and squeezed her into my chest, "You are adorable when you are flustered."

"I'm glad you're enjoying it," she mumbled.

I raised her chin and kissed her once.

"Do not worry, Kasey. You are special to me the way you are. Do not try to change yourself or hide who you are because you are afraid of what I might think."

Her eyes glazed over, and she hastily looked down.

I raised her chin once again.

"Besides, we are supposed to be predestined lovers, remember? We are stuck with each other with all the good and the bad." I grinned from ear to ear.

She did not. The notion of our fated love bothered her. Did she fear committing to me as she did with Teal? I leaned in to embrace and kiss her. The kiss she returned was cold.

## 13. Kasey's Gifts

"It is nice to finally be done with school. I am looking forward to returning home," Madhu looked at the intricate opal jewelry through the glass. We had gone shopping down in Palma, me for Christmas, and she gathering some last items she wanted before she left Spain.

"I'm going to miss you so much. My second semester is not going to be the same without you." I gave her a puppy dogface.

"You too, girl. But you have Dion to keep you busy." Her smiled widened. "How is that going?"

"It's okay. That's what I'm trying to figure out here. What to get him for Christmas?" I worried.

"You know, here in Spain, they only give gifts to the children on the Epiphany." Madhu informed.

"Yes, yes, but back home we give gifts to the ones closest to us. I feel weird not getting at least something small for him or his brothers or the Castillo's." I shrugged my shoulders.

"I do not understand you strange Americans. You are not Christian, correct? Why do you celebrate Christmas then?"

Our cultural differences amused me.

"I never really thought of it that way. Over there the holiday season is big. It's easy to get wrapped up into it. My family never did any of the religious stuff that went along with it, just the fun stuff."

"Bizarre."

"Before we leave Palma I need to stop by the post office to mail my brother and parent's Christmas gifts."

"Are you sending anything to Teal?" Her tone exuded to a hint of suspicion.

Madhu is a great friend to me here in Deia. I couldn't imagine telling Dion about the drama that was going on back home with my parents, Nolan, and Teal. I told her everything, especially everything about Teal and me.

"I feel guilty he's done so much for Nolan. I found a small canvas painting of the sun rising here in Mallorca over the ocean and the cliffs. It is beautiful. It would go well in his apartment. I stuck it in Nolan's package with a post card that said, Thanks for taking care of my brother Merry Christmas."

Mahdu chuckled.

"Do you think it was too much? Should I not send him anything?"

The past few days the package caused me angst. I must have wrapped and un-wrapped it five times taking the picture out and placing it back in. I wanted to give it to him, but I didn't want him to think anything of it.

"Sounds harmless enough. We will see when he gets it." She was skeptical.

"What do I get Dion?" I threw my hands in the air frustrated.

"Mmmm...girl, you got me. The boys' richer than the queen." She always exaggerated.

"Nothing I will give him will be as cool as anything he already has."

We walked out of the jewelry store.

"Maybe something sentimental, love-y dove-y?" she suggested.

I shook my head disgusted, "No."

"While you think, I am going to stock up on more clothes." She headed for the chic clothing store across the street.

That's when I noticed the small dark store with a purple door and half moon on it. The sign flashed, *Experiencia Religiosa*. Maybe he would like something of that nature. I crossed the street and entered the dimly lit store. The strong incense smell burned the inside of my nostrils. Trinkets and artifacts cluttered every shelf. A mixture of dream catchers and wind chimes hung throughout the ceiling. There were iconic statues everywhere, from Jesus, Saints, to dragons and fairies. Candles, potions, crystals, and books galore, were scattered around with no rhyme or reason.

It was a place of comfort to me. Here in this little shop old secular religious items co-existed with modern earthy occult trinkets. Like Dion and I. It gave me hope that he and I could make it work.

## Men of the Cave

A young woman with a long flowing red skirt, pale skin, and black long hair came from around the counter and asked in Spanish if I needed any help. I replied I was browsing.

The predominantly Catholic section was located at the back. I glanced over the statues and saw it. A grey marble stone carved with a cave and seven men lying in various positions, sleeping. The golden plate at the bottom read "*The men of the cave.*" They are celebrities in the religious world, and now I was somehow a part of it. Deciding the statue would look great in my room, I turned to head for the counter and saw the Christmas display. I found what I needed for his brothers. I hit a couple of more stores before Madhu called me.

"Girl, where are you?" she asked.

"I'm outside a shoe store, you?"

"I am ready. Meet me at my car, and we will head back."

I wasn't too far from her parked car. As I approached, she noticed my load of shopping bags.

"Accomplished much?" She gave me a hand with my bags.

"Everything," I said with a big smile.

"Good. Let us go eat. It is the last time I get to eat at Fernando's and Beatriz's restaurant."

Dion stopped by to pay his farewells to Madhu. We all ate lunch together. Fernando made Madhu her favorite meal broad slices of hake flavored with a Galician sauce called *ajada*. It was divine. We laughed, reminisced, and drank wine. It was the perfect ambiance. After we hugged several times, Madhu left to catch her plane later that evening. After the festivities, Dion followed me up to my room.

"Did a little shopping, did we?" He commented about the bags on my bed.

"Yes, I finally finished Christmas shopping. I can't believe how beautiful Deia is decorated for the holiday. Back home it's not decked out like it is here. There's two or three nativity sets wherever you turn." I sat on the floor in front of my bed taking out the tape, scissors, and wrapping paper.

"Yes, they do an exquisite job here. The nativities are taken seriously."

"I can't wait to experience Christmas in this little village." Even though I never participated in the Christian aspect of Christmas, my family decorated with green garlands and partook in the gift exchange. Not sure how my parents really felt about the holiday, I had a suspicion that the gift exchange was to appease Nolan and me.

"Be prepared for weeks of celebrations and night long feasts." He walked over to the statue of *"The men of the cave"* sitting on the windowsill.

"Nice statue."

"Thanks. I picked it up in Palma. Would you like to help me? You could wrap your brother's gifts."

"You bought my brothers Christmas gifts!"

"Nothing much. Just a little something. I wanted to. Is that okay?" I began to doubt my decision.

"I suppose, sure. What could you possibly have gotten them?" His bewildered expression was cute.

I took out four boxes that each held a crystal glass Christmas tree ornament. Inside each ornament was an elaborate wooden carving.

"I got John the glass ball with the medieval jester inside, for Martin I bought the ball with the sword in the stone scene."

Dion took the glass balls in his hands and stared at them. He smiled. Then I continued.

"For Antony I got the glass ball with the whale fluke sticking out of the water, and for Max I bought the one with the woman by the stream getting some water. She has a crescent moon on her forehead. I know his wife's name meant moon. Do you think he'll like it?"

Dion took Antony's and Max's glass balls in his hands. His grin faded. He stared at the gifts pensively.

"I love you Kasey," he blurted out.

"What?" I wondered if this was a practical joke.

"You are the most genuine person. I...I utterly love everything about you. Your thoughtfulness and dedication to detail, your constant worrying, your openness. We are perfectly perpendicular to each other, my little gypsy." He put the gifts down and kneeled by my side.

"Here...now...I'm supposed to tell you I love you according to John's vision?" I asked shocked and not ready to reciprocate.

He chuckled, "Relax, you do not say it now. John's vision was not like this. I wanted you to know what I thought." He kissed my forehead. "I know your affection for me, no worries."

At that moment Catalina knocked on the bathroom door and walked into my room with her typical pissed off expression. I never thought that I would welcome her presence as much as I did at that very moment. She sat down at the end of my bed wearing a blood red shirt with a black and white plaid skirt. I overheard a phone conversation between her and James earlier; they planned a date tonight.

"You were right." She glanced down at her hands. "I spoke to a friend whose dad…ummm, how do you say…works with the dead?"

"You mean he's the town's mortician." I gave her the words in English.

"Yes, he asked some questions for me. You were right about Elena." She looked down, ashamed. "But dead wrong about James." She finished nasty, then left the room. I looked at Dion, we both shrugged our shoulders about her. Somehow, she and James managed to avoid running into us or any of the Kleon brothers. They were keeping their romantic involvement secretive.

"So, if I get the same reaction from your brothers as I did from you when they open their gifts. I'd say they were hits," I smiled at him.

He laughed, relieved.

"The winter solstice is three days away." I brought up a touchy subject.

"Yes, yes it is."

"Are Sam and James going to come to the house?" I asked.

"Probably," he answered.

"I want to be there." I finished wrapping one gift and grabbed another.

"No." He sat on the bed.

"Dion, please be reasonable. I want to be there. Maybe I can help."

"Absolutely not, how could you possibly help?" He asked.

"I don't know, I can't bear the thought that something horrible could happen and I won't even know."

He stood and pulled me up towards him. I wrapped my arms around his waist, and he imitated me. His smile was a painting I could stare at forever.

"It is going to be all right. When it is over, I shall come for you. I promise," he said.

I moved my eyes away from his. "What if you…what if you don't come." I barely got the words out.

"I will. Of course I will." He pressed his warm lips to my forehead.

"Plus, you have to go to the fire jumping. It is fun. You will enjoy it."

"Fire jumping?" I questioned.

"It is a tradition here to jump over a small bon fire on the night of the winter solstice for a year of good health. It is a pagan ritual they still uphold."

"Can't I stay with you at your house?"

"No, you are going to go with the Castillo's and the whole village down to the ruins for the celebration. I would prefer you in a very public place."

I pouted and laid my head on his soft cotton tee. He rocked me. His big strong arms felt like a protective covering that nothing could get through. I looked up at him then raised myself on my toes. He smiled and leaned in to kiss me.

We locked ourselves into a passionate waltz of lips. Then I placed my hand around his neck and began kissing him with small quick kisses down from his cheek all the way to the sides of his neck. He did the same to me. I moved my hand from his waist and gently caressed his firm butt. He smiled at my gesture and resumed his earlier position on my lips. He ran his fingers feather-like down my spine stopping at the eve of my lower back. His other hand touched my upper right thigh.

"How is your abrasion?" he whispered.

"It's coming along," I said, rubbing noses with him. "Would you like to see?"

He glanced down at his hand and my hip. Then he leaned in and continued to kiss me with intensity. I maneuvered his hand on my hip and slid it under my shorts onto the very same spot. He jerked it out and backed up.

"Kasey, if I were not...I cannot. I should get going." He stumbled stepping back from me.

I nodded and exhaled. "I understand."

He took a deep breath and rubbed his hands through his hair.

"I shall see you later tonight for dinner."

"Yes, later."

He kissed me and left.

Disappointed, I needed a cool down. A good run. Even though the crisp air outside started to have a nip, I put on my grey running pants with a white tank and sports bra. I was going to push it hard, so I knew I would get sweaty even if the temperature outside was in the forties. I grabbed my little black purse and placed my travel journal in it.

I figured I should take the opportunity to run to the ruins and jot down some notes about them. The late afternoon was perfect, the wind cool, and the salty air refreshing. I misjudged the distance. The ruins were further than expected. I needed the break after the long journey. Sitting on the cold ground with my journal in hand, I drew the formations that the rubble of stones made.

The sun, a few hours before descending, allowed the temperature to drop sequentially as it made it's way toward the horizon. The still forest lent itself to a perfect tranquil afternoon. I broke my concentration from my drawing to look up at the position of the rubble, and there stood Sam and James. An eerie chill traveled through my body. They resembled wax statues with their eyes fixed on me. I stared back, closed my journal, and stood.

"Hello Kasey," Sam started.

"I was just gathering my stuff and going," I sputtered.

He puckered his lips. "Uhhh, do not leave on our account."

I placed my journal into my black bag without ever taking my eyes off them. My heart pounded with harsh quick beats. I couldn't breathe. I wasn't sure what to expect, Sam intimidated me. Had they followed me out here? But why?

"You know, Kasey, all you are doing, is allowing Dion to suffer for all time." Sam said.

"You think you know, but you don't know anything about us."

"Are you telling me I do not know what a siren like you is doing to my brother? You think you know our world, woman?"

"I know about the immortals," I said.

"You know! What do you know? You know nothing of our world. Be very careful, Kasey. Our world is not meant for humans."

I was frightened out here without any one to help me. I didn't know how to get away. They were men with great power, and I was merely a human. I closed my eyes and hoped that John and Martin would see this happening.

"I wish for you to leave my brothers be. I will pay you to go and never come back into their world." Sam took a few steps forward.

"Why? What do I matter?"

"You have no idea what you will do to him once you are gone. Your love will be his destruction. Is that what you really want?" James asked.

"Kasey, I am offering them salvation from this dreadful existence. With you around, you have given Dion something to live for. He will never choose to end his life unless you were dead." Sam lifted his eyebrows.

"Why are you so hell-bent on ending their lives?" I sounded a lot braver than I felt. "And if I don't leave? Then what, Sam? Are you going to make sure I end up dead?" I said the words not thinking. Was I stupid? I just gave him an open invitation to kill me.

"Kasey, do not be ridiculous. However, I do believe you might need some persuasion. You have seen what James can do, now let me show you what I can do." He crouched ready to sprint. Then his body fell lifeless to the ground. From it, a transparent cloud lifted like fog.

I took a step back.

The mist transformed into the shape of a ghost tiger, huge and vicious. The tiger charged with a furious growl.

I ran with a shriek. Every muscle in my body pushed as hard as it could. The sporadic Juniper trees made it a tricky obstacle course. I took quick glances back. The grunts and heaves from the ghost tiger sounded close in pursuit. I sped up, pumping even harder to get away. I took sharp turns and quick cuts to avoid the hard wrinkled trunks of the trees. All of a sudden, I became aware that the panting sounds stopped. Was he still behind me?

Not taking the chance I did not slow down. I took a hasty look backwards and saw nothing. I didn't like this. Not knowing Sam's whereabouts was worse than knowing he was behind me.

The impact to my cheek came unexpectedly. I felt the sting of a scrape the tree left on my cheek. I grabbed hold of the tree trunk to steady myself. I needed a moment to catch my breath. The only one panting was me. Then something poked my shin. It wasn't a sharp sting, simply a prick of annoyance. A small stick about five inches poked my leg again then fell to the ground.

It was as if that stick relayed a message to all the other sticks. In a surreal way, around my legs, every small twig on the ground began floating up, swirling like a tornado with me in the center. Like a magician's curtain, the sticks covered my whole body. One after another, the pricks came with constant, never-ending stabs like a swarm of bee stings.

My hands flapped I swatted away the brushwood. What I saw next, made me stop my panicked dance. James stood a few feet away, his face concentrated. His hand was up at chest level, and his fingers twitched.

"Stop this, please!"

The jabs stopped, and the sticks fell to the ground. His hand lowered.

"Take Sam's warning, Kasey. Leave my brothers alone."

"How could you do this to them? They don't want to die." I stepped back in case I needed to run again.

James' fingers twitched again. He elevated my body a good five feet from the ground. Paralyzed, I had no control. He pushed his hand forward, and shoved my back into the tree.

"Leave tonight for America and do not return!" he demanded.

The pressure tightened on my chest. Feeling pressed like a sandwich it was hard to breathe.

The roar of the tiger bellowed through the forest. From twenty feet ahead, the animal raced toward us. I hit the ground. Not allowing James a second to show off another of his tricks, I lifted myself and ran. Somehow, the ghost tiger jumped ahead onto my path. It snarled. I turned to avoid running right into him. It seemed I'd never be able to out run the spirit tiger.

I came to a large tree trunk with some bushes surrounding its base. Slipping between the bushes, I stood still behind the tree. It was difficult to keep my wild breathing under control. I listened for any sounds of the tiger and heard soft foots steps on the other side of the tree. I crouched down into the bushes for more coverage in the prickly shrub. An icy breath blew onto my shoulder and grazed my cheek. A whisper seemed to come from the leaves.

"Kaaassseeyy," it hissed. Something soft, cold, and smooth slithered across my shoulders. Fearful, I glanced down. A lucid serpent glided diagonally on my body.

I let out a pleading cry. "No, please." I threw myself onto my back and scooted backwards on my hands and feet. A familiar growl echoed, and the snake transformed back into the tiger. Stumbling to my feet, I sprinted with the tiger right behind me. I ran forward, but took a quick glance backward. A paw lunged inches from me. A sharp sting ached across my back. Then there was no ground left for me to run on. Screaming, I descended off the cliff, toward the rocks.

## 14. Dion's Plea

"Diiiooonnn!!" The blood curdling screams barreled through the silent house. Antony and I were playing a racing game. We dropped our controllers and ran for the kitchen. The twins entered the room, still screaming my name.

"What is wrong?" I pressed.

"It is Kasey. It is not good, Dion." Martin looked panicked.

"What did you see?" I screamed at him.

"She is running in the forest, scared and screaming." Martin said.

"What? That is the present. John, what did you see?" I tensed.

He shook his head and his eyes glazed over. "Oh, Dion I am truly sorry."

I grabbed him by his shirt mad with desperation. "What did you see?"

"Her body at the bottom of a cliff." Tears streamed down his eyes.

"Nooooo! No, that is the future, which has not happened. We have to find her. Now!" I yelled at my brothers.

"Dion, I am going to call my friends they will help us. Martin, John, can you focus on a location?" Antony gripped my shoulder. "Remember the future cannot be changed."

He headed out the door.

"Maybe, but we must at least try to help her." I ran my hands through my hair. This could not be happening. This could not be real. Why her? Why now? The universe made no sense she is to be my intended. Outside, Antony chirped loudly, within a few minutes every type of bird that lived in the forest surrounded us. Our pool deck looked like a quilt of multi colored feathers. There were Black Storks, Scops Owl, Little Bitterns, a Black Vulture, and Eleonora's Falcon.

"My friends I ask a favor of you. There is a girl with hair as red as fire. She is either running through the forest or has fallen over a cliff. Please find her and tell me of her location."

The Scops Owl resembled the bark of a tree. Its stone rough colors helped it hide into the forest's natural landscape. The Owl flew down with wings wide and landed next to Antony on the lounge chair. She spoke to him with a series of chirps and whoos. Antony translated, "She says she saw the girl earlier at the ancient ruins."

With that, all his feathered friends flew up in a massive dark cloud dispersing through the great sky.

"I am sorry Dion we are too upset, we cannot get a location." Martin said irritated.

"I am going to the ruins, meet me there."

The vibrations rattled everything in my proximity as I broke the sound barrier. I normally tried not to do that as to not raise suspicion on us, but at this very second I did not care. I needed to get to her before John's vision came true. When I arrived at the ruins, Kasey's little black purse lay on the ground in the middle of the stones. Sam's lifeless body lay ten feet away.

The rage over came me, and I knew he was behind this. The cliffs were to the north. Just as I approached, James stood at the edge of the cliff. His fingers twitched. Then Kasey's body appeared, floating in air, over the cliff's edge. He gently lowered her to the ground.

I slowed and approached her lifeless body. With great care, I placed my hand under her head.

"Kasey," I said to her. There was no response. I brought my ear to her face and felt a faint airflow exiting her lips. A slow stream of blood from a cut on her forehead trickled down, and her cheek was rosy pink from an abrasion. Her eyes twitched with pain.

"Dion! I am truly sorry. We never meant to hurt her. He was supposed to only scare her." James said panicked.

"Get away from her!" I raged.

I picked up her body carefully and cradled her close to me. She made no sounds but her facial expression became that of pain. She experienced some sort of ache.

"Stay with me Kasey. Hold on my love." I whispered in her ear. Afraid the pressure of my high speed could crush or break any bones she might have broken on her fall. I reduced my velocity by half and headed for Max's clinic. She let out a low cry of pain. I kept whispering into her ear, "Just stay with me

Kasey. It is not much longer now." I had to hurry. Max would not be able help her if she died.

The clinic glass doors, with their white letters that read "Dr. Maxamillian Kleon," were locked. A light shined down the hall. I pounded on the door with my foot. If he arrived a minute later I would have kicked the glass door down, but Max came running to the door straight away. Opening the door, he asked. "What happened?"

"She fell off a cliff," I answered.

"What! Go to the first room lay her down. Is she breathing?"

We ran to the first exam room. I placed her body down on the cushioned exam table. Max lit the room with the pale florescent lights.

"She is barely breathing," I informed him.

"Go get her an oxygen mask, now!" As I left the room, his hand began to glow. I returned with the oxygen materials, positioned the mask over her face, and hooked up the tube. Max looked grave.

"She has a concussion, but worse, her cervical spine is fractured in three different places. I sensed severe nerve damage. Her ribs are pressing against her lungs."

"Ohhh…God…" I bent down, placing my hand to her forehead.

"Dion, I can reposition her lungs back in place to get her breathing again, but if the nerves broke off completely and detached near her dorsal spinal root…" He stared at Kasey. "She might not walk."

Sick, I felt an ache all through my body. I looked at Max.

"Please, do what you can. She is in pain." I urged. He nodded.

I could not stand the thought that she was currently suffering. At that moment, we heard the door to the clinic and Antony, John, Martin, and James walked into the exam room.

"Let us get started." Antony said taking his spot next to Max.

James, Martin, and John stayed by the foot of the exam table.

"What is James doing here?" I growled. The anger consumed me and revenge was all I wanted. James gave me a regretful expression I did not buy.

"Dion, I did not do this. We were only trying to scare her away from you. Believe me, I want to make sure that she is all right."

Growling through my teeth, I grumbled. "You have no business here."

"Dion!" Max snapped. "I need your focus here, not there."

His hard command caused me to snap out of my anger.

"What do you need?" Antony asked Max.

"Get me a towel and a scalpel." Max ordered. Antony began rummaging through the cupboards.

"Dion, help me flip her. Easy now."

We rolled her body so that she lay on her stomach. There was an echo of gasps as we all saw the three slashes across her back with some bloodstains. Sam did this to her. There was no doubt he pushed her off. Angst and rage battled inside of me. I pulled her ponytail away from her face and positioned her arms down at her sides.

Max whispered a prayer under his breath. He pulled the drawer under the sink and pulled out a pair of surgical scissors. He took the scissors, cut straight up her ripped shirt and bra, and then cut the straps off. He stretched her white tank top off her shoulders and off her sides exposing her back. He took his left hand and placed it around her neck it glowed with bright yellow rays. Then her back began to glow in the same manner.

"Dion, you do not have to watch this," Max said.

"I am not leaving her." I placed my hand over her head and stroked her hair with my thumb.

"Remember she will never feel a thing," Max reassured. "Antony the scalpel."

Antony handed Max the scalpel. Then Max cut a perfect line into her flesh from her neck to the bottom of her back. The incision did not bleed Max had the ability of controlling the blood flow and keeping it within her body. I held my breath and could not swallow due to the lump in my throat. Max put the bloody scalpel down then with the same hand; he parted her flesh using only his thumb and pointer finger. The incision needed to be wide enough for him to slip his hand through it.

I turned my head and closed my eyes. Over hundreds of years, I watched him perform countless surgical procedures. Never did I care for the medical profession, but it by no means bothered me. Tonight was different. I could not bear the thought that Kasey was undergoing this. She did nothing to deserve this. It was merely because she was with me. How could I have left her unprotected? I never imagined a brother of mine capable of such a thing.

I opened my eyes as Max inserted his hand into the widen incision.

After rummaging around her insides, he said. "Her lungs are good. You can remove the mask. I have her breathing normal."

Antony detached the oxygen mask from her face. I squeezed her hand. An ache pierced my stomach as clicks resonated through the silent exam room.

"Her bones are in place. Now I am going to start to repair the nerves."

Martin stepped back after the third crack; he rocked from side to side. Time never moved more slow. It took him numerous minutes or so. As his hand passed the damaged areas in her spine, his fingers worked to heal the tissues, muscles, and nerves.

When his hand reached her lower back, his eyebrows furrowed.

"What is wrong?" I asked.

"This is the area I worried about. She has two nerves still attached by a miracle."

"Does this mean she will walk?" I asked.

"Give me two seconds and I will let you know." Max's fingers worked. He concentrated. "They healed nicely. She will walk."

I sighed. My legs gave out and I bent next to the table. Then I kissed her forehead.

Max pulled his hand out of her body and wiped it on the towel. With that same hand glowing, he passed it over her incision gliding his fingers skillfully on the opening. He began from the bottom of her back to the top, ever so slow. After his radiating fingers passed over the cut, it vanished. When the entire incision and the three slashes on her skin were gone, he removed both his hands from her body.

"Flip her over." Max commanded. I placed my hands under her shoulder and rib cage then lifted her up. I moved my hand onto her chest holding her clothing in place to keep her decent. I could feel her tender breasts beneath my fingertips. Antony rolled her towards him and we laid her onto her back.

Max placed his glowing hand on her forehead. The bleeding cut disappeared. He then ran his thumb down her cheek and healed any reminisce of the scrape. Max went over to the sink and scrubbed his hands. She began to moan.

"Max..." I found it hard to get the words out, "I cannot even thank..." I shook my head and swallowed hard.

"I know Dion...I know," Max reassured.

"Dion, we know what she means to you," John placed his hand on my shoulder.

"She is special to you brother, she is special to all of us," Antony smiled.

"We would give our lives for her," Martin stepped up.

I had not notice that James had stepped out of the room, but he reentered with a blanket for Kasey. We laid the blanket over her, body this woke her into consciousness. She looked around the room confused. I grabbed her hand and squeezed it twice.

"What…" she tried to ask, but her voice was hoarse and raspy. She lifted her head.

"Get her some water." Max ordered Martin.

He left the room.

"Take it easy Kasey, relax." Max placed his hand on her forehead. She rested her head back, but still looked concerned.

"How do you feel?" Max asked.

"Strange…I'm really sore." She looked around bewildered.

"Do me a favor and move your legs."

She immediately looked alarmed. Kasey rocked her legs back and forth.

"You will feel stiff, as if your body underwent a rigorous work out. Before you walk make sure to stretch your spine and legs." Max instructed her.

Martin re-entered the room with a plastic cup of water. He handed it to me and I brought it to Kasey's lips. She reached up and tried to take hold of it herself, but her hand trembled.

"What happened?" she asked, looking at James. He avoided her eyes and looked down ashamed. "I was being chased and then…"

"You fell off a cliff. Max mended your spine. It was fractured," I informed her.

"What? Really?" She became anxious.

"We will give you some space." Max gestured for the others to leave the room.

They left, and I bent close to Kasey's face. I leaned in and kissed her tenderly.

"Will I be alright?" She asked concerned.

"Yes. He was able to heal your spine completely. You scared us. For a second we didn't think you would walk again." I kissed her forehead.

"I can't believe I'm not in pain." She said amazed.

Max entered the room. "Pardon me, Kasey but you have been through quite an ordeal today. I would suggest you rest for a while." Max dimmed the lights.

"Dion, why not go with your brothers and look for Sam? I shall stay here with Kasey, she will be fine."

I kissed the back of her hand then I kissed her lips. I whispered into her ear, "I love you." Then I squeezed her hand and walked out of the room so that she might sleep.

## 15. Kasey It's Time

I didn't want Dion to leave me, but my body craved sleep. He left and before Max closed the door, I called his name.

"Do you need something?" he asked.

"No, no, I...I wanted to thank you for saving my life. I know you don't particularly like me...I just wanted to say thanks."

"My dear Kasey, I am truly sorry if this is what I have led you to believe. It is not that I do not like you. You are a fine girl."

"I always thought you didn't want me and Dion together."

He confused me.

"In a way I do not. You have to understand, I know what my brother is going to go through when this period of bliss is over. Cyra and I were in absolute ecstasy. So in love, so much passion, and then in a fraction of a second she was gone. There is not a day in a thousand years that I do not yearn for her touch. Some days I wake up in the morning, and I swear I can smell her floral scent next to me. There is nothing more powerful than love and nothing more painful. I would never wish this eternity of suffering, of longing to be with her some day, on any man, much less my own brother. My wishes were for him to avoid this pain. But I suppose love is unavoidable."

I could see the suffering in his worn eyes. Would this be Dion after I'm long passed?

"Max, if you could turn back the hands of time, knowing what you know now. Would you have allowed yourself to love Cyra?"

His face became blank as if he was mentally reminiscing. Then he half smirked and nodded.

"I would take a thousand years of suffering again for even one day, one kiss, of hers." And with that, he left the room.

It must be hard for him to have such control, such discipline of his emotions. Even though sometimes he seemed callous toward his brothers, I saw why they all admired him and allowed him to be their father figure. He was young, merely twenty-five, when God robbed him of his human life, but Max exemplified the wisdom much like that of an elder.

I couldn't help to think of what was to become of Dion and me. I would continue to age and then one day pass on to the next stage. That would never happen to him. I wondered if two soul mates agonized for each other until the day they were able to be together. Was Cyra longing for her Max wherever her spirit resided? I must accept destiny for what it is. I needed to believe that fate had a plan a reason for what it did. I could not think of the suffering Dion would endure when I passed, or I would never fully embrace the love intended for us. Exhausted, I fell into a heavy sleepy state.

I awoke from my sleep, and it seemed like years passed. Dion sat in a chair watching me. I smiled.

"Hello beautiful." He reciprocated my smile.

"What time is it?"

"It is ten o'clock in the evening," he replied.

"Hmmm…" I stretched. My neck was still stiff, "It's so late."

I sat up. I realized gravity allowed my clothing to fall downward. Immediately I placed my hand over my breasts, holding in place my tank top and sports bra. Shredded and bloodied, my white tank hardly covered me. I noticed the cold chill on my bare back. Shocked by these revelations I asked, "What happened to my top?"

Dion, whose facial expression illustrated that he was enjoying the fact I was half-topless, explained, "Max cut it off in order to properly work on your spine."

Goosebumps spread through my skin. I shuttered at the thought.

"Did he have to cut me open?"

"Wide open." Dion grinned.

I sighed. "Gross. Why couldn't he just touch me and heal?"

"Kasey, this is not Hollywood. It does not work quite like that."

"What do you mean?"

"In order for Max to heal a body part he must physically touch that body part. If a bone is broken he must touch that bone so that the bone can begin to heal, then he heals the muscle, then the skin. If it is an organ he must place his hand on the organ."

"I can't believe I don't feel a thing other than sore." I said dumbfounded.

"He has an amazing gift," Dion said.

Looking down I flushed. Embarrassed I asked, "Did everyone see me like this?"

He smiled big, "Yes, but you were always properly covered up. I promise."

That didn't make me feel any better about his brothers seeing me so bare. He stood and walked over to me. I'd never seen him look so unkempt, his hair disheveled and messy. He looked adorable in his tight black tee shirt with faded ripped jeans. He came and stood by my side. I lifted my shirt a tad higher, due to my awkward state. I didn't look at him. He took his hand and softly caressed my forearm up to my bare shoulder. Then he took his thumb and with a feather touch, passed it across my shoulder blade, down the middle of my back outlining my spine. He stopped at the very bottom of my lower back. A tingly sensation traveled through parts of my body and my skin filled itself with goose bumps. He reached down and kissed the lower part of the back of my neck. I let out a heavy breath.

"My sincerest apologies for what my brothers did to you," he said in a soft voice.

"You don't have to apologize for your brothers actions."

"Still, I should have been there to protect you."

"You saved my life. You did protect me." I looked at him with a kind smile. He leaned down and kissed me lightly. I let his hand explore all of my back as our lips continued a rhythmic dance. With his other hand, he caressed the opposite shoulder. For a split second, I thought about letting the hand on my chest let go of the clothing it was holding up. Before I could act on the thought, he stopped and stepped back.

"Here, I took a tee shirt from John for you to wear." He placed a burgundy tee shirt in my lap.

"Oh, thank you."

I must have been overly eager in my thank you, because he chuckled.

"I will turn around so you can change." He then walked back toward the chair and faced the wall.

The tee shirt had a big recycling triangle in the middle. Inside the triangle was a river with fish in it. After I finished I said. "Okay I'm good, interesting shirt."

"Sorry, John grabbed it," he said taking no blame in the matter.

I got off the exam table slow and steady. Even though I felt fine, I was somewhat freaked about the medical procedure I underwent. Dion came over to me at once. He must have thought the same, unsure how I would do on my feet. I grabbed hold of his arm and steadied myself for a second.

"I'm okay," I said letting go and stepped forward. I twisted and turned my upper body in a stretch. My spine cracked several times. As I passed the sink, I took a quick glance at my reflection. It mortified me. "Oh, God. I look horrible."

I rubbed my cheeks for they were unusually pale. I pulled out my band that held an un-kept ponytail. I let my hair fall loose.

"You look like you fell off a cliff today, but otherwise still beautiful," Dion said putting his hand on my back and kissing my head. He placed a large grey coat over my shoulders.

Dion locked up the clinic for Max and we headed for his house. The night was dreadfully wintry. Always a Florida girl, the forty-degree night air sent a chill down to every bone in my body. He cranked the heat in his car for me. Winter was on its way. As we walked into his gorgeous art-deco mansion, the aroma of something delicious traveled right to the core of my stomach. It rumbled loudly and shocked me.

"Hungry?" he asked amused.

"I think I am." I headed for the kitchen.

John, Martin, and Antony were in the kitchen. The twins munched on some Empanadas. Antony ate a salad.

"Kasey, you have come back from the dead!" John came over and gave me a great big bear hug and kiss on the cheek. Then Antony and Martin also greeted me with kisses on my cheek.

"I can't thank you guys enough for all you did."

"You do not have to mention it," Antony said.

"No worries it is part of the day job." John beamed.

Dion and I sat down and grabbed two brown crispy Empanadas. Before I picked mine to bite into it Antony offered, "Kasey I made enough salad for two if you would like that instead. It is southwest so it has spicy beans and peppers."

"Oh, that sounds much better. Thank you Antony." He was strange, but kind, and down to earth. Dion grabbed my empanada and placed it on his plate. Antony proceeded to prepare me a plate of salad. Layna entered the room with her casual stride. She placed herself at Antony's feet.

"Did Sam ever resurface?" I remembered the tiger in the forest.

"Martin and John received a vision of him leaving Deia and in his condo in Palma, but when we went there he was gone," Antony answered.

"Do you think he'll be back?" I worried.

"Oh, he will return, but I do not think before the winter solstice," Dion said.

"Where's Max?" I asked noting that we were a brother short.

"He and James have been privately talking for the past three hours," Martin answered.

"If he is confessing then they will be in there for the next three months," John said hypercritical.

"Do you think we can trust him?" I asked doubtful.

At that moment, Max and James entered the room.

"I think we can. He is a Kleon brother and welcome here." Max put his arm around James approvingly. I swallowed; embarrassed that he heard my question.

"I am sorry, Kasey, for everything. I never meant to hurt you. We wanted to scare you off. I truly am sorry," James said attempting to be humble.

I nodded, but looked away, remembering how he pressed me against that tree.

Dion spoke grimly. "I am not ready to forget."

James shook his head. "I understand. When the time is right then."

"Kasey, how does your spine feel?" Max approached me. His hand glowed as he scanned my back. I couldn't look at his face. My cheeks burned with embarrassment.

"I feel fine, thanks." I sputtered quickly.

"What about Sam? What is his plan?" asked Antony in a serious tone.

"Sam is not a terrible man. He is simply lost. I think in his mind he figures he is offering a form of salvation to his brothers. He does not want you to suffer this immortal life anymore."

"What about him? Why does he not want death for himself? He suffers as much, if not more, than any of us?" John said sully.

"He figures there is no hope for him to ever have redemption, so immortality is the best choice he has." James grabbed an empanada.

"Whatever happens, we will be ready," Max said, ending that conversation. "James is going to stay here with us until he decides otherwise," Max informed the clan.

Dion leaned into me, "Are you finished eating? I would like to show you something."

I followed him out of the kitchen and into the hallway by the front door. He grabbed a black leather jacket from the closet, and helped me into it. He took locks of my hair from under the jacket and un-tucked my red curls. Only the tips of my fingers stuck out from the sleeves. Like a girl in her daddy's jacket.

"Where are we going?" I asked as he put on his grey jacket.

"Up to see the stars." He grabbed my sleeve and led me outside. Hidden from plain sight, behind tall bushes, a steel spiral black staircase led up to the house's flat roof.

The tranquil air carried no breeze tonight. It was exceedingly frigid. Winter was moving into Spain and the island of Mallorca.

The leather jacket did a stellar job keeping the parts it covered warm. The flat roof was decent big in size with a ruble floor. A two-foot boarder wall, made up the edge. The black night sky lit up with what looked like a thousand little Christmas lights. The ghost colored moon was in its waxing gibbous stage. That meant that it would be at full the night of the winter solstice. In the middle of the roof, bolted to the floor, a telescope with a metal case covering stood in isolation. Dion went up to it and took the covering off.

"Is that a refractor telescope?" I asked as he looked through the lens. Raised with a mother whose hobby is to watch the constellations and planetary movements through the houses and signs of Astrology, I knew something about telescopes.

He popped up shocked and looked at me. "Why yes, yes it is. Oh Kasey," he said excited, "you are most certain the woman for me."

Laughing, I looked down the beautiful pool deck, all lit up. I stared out into the dark ocean in all its vastness. I reflected on my near death experience. I exhaled in mere gratitude that I was still breathing. If my human existence ended today, I'd be stuck as an unfinished ghost. The thought of spending an eternity regretting something I should have done a long time ago disrupted the pit of my stomach. It is time.

"Are you ready?" Dion looked through the lens of the telescope and fidgeted with the knobs and focus.

"Sure," I walked towards him. "What are we looking at?"

He stepped aside and let me look through the lens. I felt his warm embrace cuddle up behind me as he wrapped his arms around my waist and pulled his body close to mine.

"It is Jupiter's four moons, the Galilean moons." His voice took on a childlike enthusiasm.

The planet looked like one of those bottles layered with colored sand. "I see the red spot!" I said, elated.

He laughed amused.

"What would you like to look at next?" he asked.

"What would you say to the sun?" I asked subtlety.

"Are you sure?" He replied.

I moved my head back and rested it on his chest. He leaned his head down to look through the lens. Our cheeks grazed and I could feel his warmth so close to me.

"Dion," I said, looking up, "I love you. With every breath I take, I love you."

He didn't look up from his telescope. He slyly smiled.

"You knew it was coming didn't you?" I accused.

He looked down and chuckled, then he looked at me, "It did not make the moment any less special to me." He kissed my cold cheek with his cold lips.

I laughed.

"Kasey," his face grew tight his eyes avoided mine, "would you like to spend the night?"

I couldn't believe he asked this of me.

"After everything that happened today I wish to hold you forever. Since forever is an unreasonable request. I would settle for at least until tomorrow." He gave me his sweet, alluring smile.

"There is nothing more I would love tonight, than to fall asleep in your arms." I replied.

He smiled and leaned in for an affectionate kiss. After a moment, he backed up.

"I promise to be a complete gentleman, but you must behave yourself."

"Of course I will behave myself. I'm not a hussy or anything like that."

"No, no, of course not. I did not mean it like that. It is that, well, you are more liberal on the matter."

"Dion, you don't have to worry. I got the message loud and clear. We will not be having sex any time soon."

"Kasey!" I didn't need the sun's light to know he blushed. The subject made him uncomfortable.

"What? I'm not going to seduce you. I'm okay with you just holding me."

He shook his head. "Here, look at the moon."

I smiled and looked through the lens.

After I could no longer stand the cold weather, we went back inside. As we headed up the stairs, John ran in from the kitchen.

"Brother, a quick minute..." He stopped, surprised to see me, "Oh Kasey, you are still here. No bother then. I shall leave you two alone."

Dion smiled at me, "What did you want?"

"Only if you are not occupied, could you go to Italy for some ice cream?" John batted his eyes in a pleading effort.

"I swear you are worse than a pregnant woman," Dion said annoyed.

"Why, Italy?" I asked.

"Ohhh," they both said.

"There is a small ice cream shop in the hills of Tuscany. Best ice cream in the world," Dion said.

"John, isn't it too cold for ice cream?" I asked.

"Ice cream is year round, it has no season," he replied.

"Okay, I will go." Dion gave in.

"Thanks brother." John ran off.

"It will take me twenty minutes at most," Dion gave me a peck on the nose.

"You are welcome to go on and make yourself at home in my room." He said as he headed downstairs.

"Would you mind if I took a shower? I could use one. Plus it would be nice to warm up."

"Not a problem at all. We each have our own bathrooms in our rooms. Help yourself to anything there." He put his coat on and walked out the door.

His room, surprisingly, didn't have a pile of cloths in sight. He painted his ceiling black with some type of specialized effect. Tiny twinkling stars shimmered throughout. It resembled a star lit sky. There were two doors side by side, the first one turned out to be an enormous walk in closet. It now housed all his piles of clothes.

In search of some clean sweat pants, I rummaged through his dresser drawers. The first drawer came up to the top of my chest. Pulling it out I found papers, notebooks, and a pile of fake passports. The second drawer held socks all in complete order. The third drawer was practically empty except for three pieces of clothing. I figured he never used these, so I helped myself to a pair of black, pull string, sweat pants.

Grabbing it, I headed for the second wooden door figuring it was the bathroom. It was a simple man's bathroom no décor, simply towels and rugs. The scorching water trickled down my body. At that moment, I realized how desperate I needed the prickly pressure of the water on my muscles. Stretching my neck and my back, I tried to work out my soreness. I was certain I spent more than the twenty minutes he took to go get the ice cream. Tying the pull string pants as tight as they could go I rolled the cuffs up. They were still baggy. I pulled John's burgundy shirt over my soaked hair. Before exiting the bathroom, I plucked the tee out a few times so that my braless breasts didn't protrude through as much.

When I opened the door all the steam from the shower exploded into his bedroom. He sat in his black loveseat with his feet up. The only light in the room came from his reading lamp in the corner.

"Feel better?" he asked.

I blushed. "Much, I needed that."

I folded my arms across my chest; I sat on the far corner of his king sized bed. With a brown bag in hand, he sat next to me. Feeling light headed, I tried to regulate my breathing. The only boy I'd ever spent the night with was Teal. My emotions confused me, how could I love Dion, yet feel agitated here in his room. He opened the bag and took out a small Styrofoam cup.

"Here see if you like it." He dipped a spoon into the ice cream and fed me. I smiled.

"Mmmmm, rich." The vibrant espresso flavor woke my senses.

He took a spoonful himself, "I was not sure if you liked espresso. It is one of my favorite."

"Good choice."

He fed me another spoonful.

"Finish up. I am going to get in a quick shower myself," he said and headed for his closet. He pulled out an item of clothing then entered the bathroom.

The view outside his window was remarkable. The land slanted downward, allowing a blanket of forest with the ocean in the distance. Looking around the room, I noticed a small stack of books next to his loveseat, I read the titles: *Astronomy Today textbook, Leopardi's Canti: poems the bilingual edition, Galileo in Rome,* and *Seven things you need to know before you date*. I snorted at the last one.

He showers like he runs, fast. The door to the bathroom opened, I faced him and inhaled forgetting to let it go. The steam around him dispersed as he stood there in a pair of cream sleeping pants. His chest glistened with the dew of the steam. His wheat colored flesh tightened perfectly muscular. He brushed back his wet dark hair. His beauty, so striking it washed away my nervousness and replaced it with desire. He smirked and I blushed. I felt sinful looking at him. I lowered my eyes and tried to avoid contact, "So," I sat on the bed.

He came to the bed and lay across it resting his head on his pillow. His chest raised and lowered gently with every breath he took. He placed his arms behind his head.

"Are you still stiff?" he asked.

If I say yes, would he give me a massage? "No."

"Good, that is good." We were both uneasy.

"So, Dion this is quite an astronomical room. When did you become such a fan of the stars?" Small talk was a better alternative to the awkwardness.

"It was Galileo who really sparked my interest in the skies. Before him, I never paid too much attention. His passion for it and fascination rubbed off."

"You mean you knew the real Galileo?"

He nodded.

I let out a long breath. "Wow," I whispered. "What I would give to have met some of the historical figures you have."

He shrugged his shoulders. "I guess I am not star struck by it. Most of them were regular people. Galileo though, was special to me. He became somewhat of a grandfather figure the little time we spent together."

I lay facing him on my own pillow.

"I guess if you're going to have someone to look up to Galileo isn't a shabby pick," I smirked.

He turned on his side to face me. He took his hand and rubbed my cheek with the back of his finger. My heart thumped with anticipation. He lifted his head and leaned in to kiss me. He was gentle and passionate, perfectly soft and intense at the right times. He placed his hand on my back and brought me close into him. My breasts pressed up against his firm bare chest. Then he reached up and held the back of my neck under my hair.

He slid his hand down gradually from the back of my neck, to my spine, and finished on my hip. He kept his hand in place for a second then proceeded to slide his hand under my tee shirt. He massaged my back running his fingers down my side almost nearly touching the sides of my breasts.

I backed up, flushed. "If you're going to touch me like that, we will end up in trouble," I took a deep breath.

He jerked away. "I am sorry Kasey...I never meant to take it as far as I did... it has been so long since..." he trailed off bothered by his actions.

I nuzzled into his body, "It's okay, I like your touch, but if we are going to keep doing this, you need to put on a shirt." My fingers skimmed down his torso.

"Seriously?" he asked with an air of innocence, signifying he had no clue how gorgeous he was.

I chuckled, "No I'm kidding. Sorry…" I let out a big nervous sigh and looked away from him.

"Are you okay Kasey?"

"Yes… it's so stupid. We aren't even going to do it tonight. I've just…I'm just…" I let out another a big sigh. I sounded like an incoherent buffoon.

He tilted my head up by my chin. "Is it the expectations thing again?"

"Yeah, I guess you can say it's that. You are some sort of great immortal and I'm…I'm just human."

He grinned. "I feel the same way. I might keep composure, but am quite nervous."

"Really?" I couldn't imagine him nervous about anything. Was he saying that to make me feel better?

"Kasey you have no idea that you are this beauty of a woman. You make Aphrodite look like a common girl."

"Dion…you're exaggerating."

"Maybe…I might be biased. I do not know what you are worried about. It has been a long time since I have done this sort of thing. I hope that I do not let you down."

"Dion you could never do that! You kiss so well you made me uncomfortable." I reassured him.

He placed his hand under my ear and caressed his thumb on my cheek. He leaned in and kissed me. "Let me know when it is too much," he whispered. Dion laid me down on my back, propped himself up over me, and slowly pressed his solid chest onto my perked up breasts. We locked lips with heated passion. How far would he take this? How far would I let him go?

## 16. Kasey and the Fire Jumping

The beam of light from the sun made it hard to keep my eyes closed for more sleep. My eyes fluttered open and tried to focus on the brightness. The pillow was soft, and I buried my cheek into it. My body squirmed under the covers. He spooned behind me. Remembering where I was, I relaxed in his arms.
"Good morning," he whispered and kissed my cheek.
Rotating, I faced him, "Good morning."
"Did you sleep well?"
"Heavenly," I replied.
He smiled. "Always good to hear."
"Your bed is comfortable and spacious," I snuggled into it.
"I am glad you like it. You are welcome to it anytime." He playfully raised one eyebrow.
"Hmmm...thank you." I reciprocated.
He propped himself on his elbow then ran his fingers through my hair, leaned in and kissed me. I ran my hand up his chest and down his shoulders caressing his back. We heard a quick knock, then his door opened.

"Dion, for breakfast we were thinking French…" Martin stopped in mid-sentence upon seeing me. "Kasey!" he squeaked like a girl. He looked embarrassed and horrified at what he thought he walked into. He turned and left slamming the door behind him. Dion sunk down into his pillow. "Bugger."

"Are you in trouble? Will they think you did something immoral?" I worried that my spending the night caused problems.

He turned his head. "No, no. They are my brothers, they know who I am, but you know how brothers can be about teasing." He sighed and sat.

"We better get up for the day. It seems my family is ready for breakfast."

"Are you the designated food runner?" I asked, amused.

"Yes, guess it is French this morning." He got out of bed and went to his closet.

"Dion, about last night…" I blushed.

"Yes, is everything all right?" He popped his head from the closet.

I wasn't sure how to put into words what I wanted to say. "I'm surprised you asked me to spend the night. You don't seem like the people in this town. Beatriz would be horrified, you seem okay with it, and I was shocked how…how close you allowed us to go last night."

He sat at the edge of the bed. "Me too," he shook his head. "I never intended for it to go as far as we did. Do you feel we did something wrong?" he worried.

"Not me, but I'm not the one who's Catholic."

"Kasey, are you questioning my faith?"

"No, I'm curious. Personally, I don't know about this stuff, other than what I have studied in a book. I guess I want to know what your thoughts are."

"Realize this. I gave my life for my God at the age of twenty. And for unexplainable reasons I was bestowed a great grace, the gift of speed. If there is anything I have learned from this lifetime, it is that everything has a reason. We have a purpose on this earth, that has not come to pass yet." He gripped my hand. "I know exactly where my faith lies, it lies with Him. I died once for Him and I would do it again. We know the world through very different eyes. We experience religion through time. It must mold to fit the customs of current society. I stayed up in the mountains of Tibet. I lived in Israel and China. I was a monk, and visited with the Mayans. As far as the rules and regulations that humans place on themselves, well that has also changed with the times. I can remember an era, where if I spoke a word to you without permission, society would punish me. We understand that customs change, and we have adapted ourselves to change with it. As far as doing what is right. I feel that you must do what your heart and soul tell you are right."

"But you still wouldn't take a girl unless you were married to her?" I asked.

"That does not feel right to me. Something so intimate so private I would never do without a marriage vow."

I squeezed his hand, understanding more about his pious world. After we both freshened up, we headed down stairs to face what felt like a panel of judges. I hid behind Dion and let him walk into the kitchen first. Antony, John, Martin, and James sat at the kitchen table attempting to keep composure. Dion sat me in one of the chairs.

"So," he said nervously, "French pastries for breakfast today. A round of cappuccinos for everyone, I presume?" His brothers nodded. He kissed my head then left for France.

"John spoke up, "Sleep well last night, Kasey?" He asked it in a comic way. His brothers sneered. He reminded me of Nolan. I knew this teasing territory came from having brothers.

"Extremely well, John thanks for asking." I played to his game. All their eyes went big with surprise. I blushed.

"Where's Max?" He was the one brother I didn't want to see. I wasn't sure if he'd like my spending the night.

Antony understood the root of my question. He gave me a smile and said, "He had a medical emergency this morning."

Relieved, I sighed. His brothers stared at me as if I were some sort of oddity. Uncomfortable, I squirmed in my seat. I think Antony noticed my uneasiness.

"So Kasey, has Dion taken you up to the telescope yet?" Antony asked.

"Yes, last night." I answered.

"That is where he takes all the girls." John gave me a pitied expression.

"Do not pay any attention to him," Antony shook his head.

"Dion has never had a girl," Martin chimed in.

I smiled. "Except his wife."

Martin, John, and Antony's shocked expressions were priceless.

"He told you about his wife!" John asked.

"Not by choice." I gave James a hard look. He avoided my stare and looked away. The others looked at each other bewildered.

"She never loved him. I do not know what Max was thinking back then, arranging that marriage. We all did a dance of celebration the day you arrived in Deia," John said.

"Why's that?" I asked.

"Oh, Dion drove us bonkers everyday about you," Martin said.

A slight giggle slipped.

"We were at that restaurant hours before you arrived. We knew you were going to get there for lunchtime. But we were not sure of the time," Martin continued. "I am surprised he did not run to St. Cloud to get a glimpse of you beforehand."

"I think Max talked him out of it. If Dion stared at you at first, it is because he could not wait to meet you. He was nervous driving you that first time," Antony said, amused.

When Dion returned I gave him a great big smile. He eyed his brothers suspiciously. He looked at me funny.

"Do not believe anything they said."

We laughed.

The French pastries and cappuccinos were the best ever. We ate breakfast, then Dion took me back home. I didn't want him to walk me inside. I thought it might cause a scandal in the Castillo household. Last time I showed up early in the morning with Dion, Beatriz lectured me on the ways a good woman should act. Her methods worked and the Catholic guilt established itself. I didn't think I did anything wrong, but Deia being a small town, the gossip is everywhere. The Castillo's were a good family, and I didn't want anyone to shame their name because of me. The situation this morning appeared worse than the other night. It was after breakfast, I was not in last night, and I was wearing Dion's clothes. The first to greet me were Rodrigo and Garcia.

"*Buenos dias* Kasey," they both said.

"Hi," I replied, and dashed for the kitchen door.

"You went running early," Garcia mentioned, before I could escape the room.

"Are you not cold in that tee-shirt?" Rodrigo noticed that I came in without a sweater, my arms crossed over my chest.

"Um…I ran hard, so I get hot easily," I lied and darted past them into the kitchen.

I jumped as I came face to face with Catalina cutting some vegetables. The minute she saw me the knife in her hand stopped. She tried to contain a smile.

"Did you spend the night at Dion's?" I hated her bluntness, an attribute we shared.

"We didn't do anything, we just slept," I blurted out unsure why I explained myself to her.

Her jaw dropped. "I am not surprised you would do something like that, but I am shocked Dion allowed it."

Her piercing comment crawled under my skin. As if I corrupted Dion or something. I went up the stairs, Fernando and Beatriz sat in the living room drinking their morning coffee. Our eyes met, and I no longer could breathe. Fernando's face tightened with a stern expression. I blushed. Beatriz looked like she failed.

"*Buenos dias* Kasey," Fernando said.

"*Buenos dias*," I replied stiff as a totem pole.

"Kasey, come in here please," Beatriz said.

I exhaled, walked into the room, and sat down in front of them.

"Kasey," Beatriz continued, "I know you come from a different world than us."

Oh, God she was giving me another lecture. Foreign to this type of parenting, I didn't know what to expect. Testing my limitations once, I ran off for an entire weekend with Teal. My parent's only comment was, "Did you have fun?"

I am eighteen now, for goodness sakes, why did I feel ashamed?

Beatriz continued, "Fernando and I are aware of our cultural differences and we want to respect your way of life, but at the same time we need to think about our way of life here." She looked at Fernando for help.

"We are not going to tell you what to do. We are asking that you keep a respectful mind of our ways and customs. Do you understand?" He asked, stressing his point.

"Clearly, *señor*. I'm sorry if I have…"

"Please, Kasey, you do not have to apologize. We understand you are who you are. That is okay, because very soon you will go back to America, and you are not our daughter." Beatriz spoke in a gentle way.

"I can't thank you enough for all you do for me and I promise I will not disrespect you guys again." I went straight for my room. I felt awful. For once in my life I was thankful that my parents didn't ever care what I did. This guilty feeling of letting the Castillo's down caused absolute misery.

******

Without any rhyme or reason to why I felt the way I did, I took a break from Dion and decided to spend my time with the family. For two days I helped preparing food and working at the restaurant. My phone vibrated in my pocket, as I stuffed octopuses. With my pinky fingers being the only ones clean, I reached in and pulled it out.

"Hi Dion," I said flustered by the phone ordeal.

"Are you alright?"

"Yes, I'm stuffing octopuses."

"Sounds like fun. Are you still under your own grounding or can I see you today?" He asked. I suspected he'd want to see me today, the winter solstice occurred tonight.

"I wasn't grounded. I thought I should spend some time with the Castillo's." I defended.

"Uh-huh. Would one hour be alright?" he asked.

"Yes, I'll make sure I'm available." I hung up the phone.

I finished the octopuses, and went upstairs to get rid of the fishy smell off. Accustomed to Dion's punctuality, when he said an hour, he meant exactly on the hour. I was in the bathroom scrubbing my arms as hard as I could with soap when he knocked on my door. Somehow, his hours seem a lot shorter than mine do.

"Come in!" I yelled. Patting my arms with a towel, I realized I'd rubbed too hard. The scrubber left red scratch marks on my whitish arms.

"Hi." I said going over to greet him.

He took one look at me and his eyes bulged out.

"What happened?" he asked.

"I'm pale, that's what." I leaned up and kissed his lips.

"Are you okay?"

"Yes, it will fade."

"You must be made of porcelain. Such a delicate human." He caressed my arms.

"So does this mean I can go over to your house tonight?" I planned on using my powers of persuasion. I fluttered my eyelids.

"And risk having you grounded again, not a chance." He sat on my bed.

"That's not what I meant and you know it." I sat down next to him, "Dion, I want to be there. You have no idea what a nervous wreck I will be knowing what's happening and not knowing what's going on. Please…" I begged.

He took a big breath, rolled his eyes around as if he pondered the thought, then kissed my lips. "No," he finally said.

"Dion," I sighed.

"Kasey absolutely not."

"I'm the one he tried to kill I have a right to be there," I pouted.

Dion tensed. "Kasey, you have no idea how betrayed I feel over what happened to you. The brother that I knew, the man who died in that cave with me, is not the same man. Sam has lost who he was. He will pay for what he did. It is our duty to ensure that he not roam the Earth as free as he does. Especially, since he is capable of committing such mortal sins."

I'd never seen Dion distraught.

"Please, don't do anything stupid. Don't let your anger over this get the better of you."

"I will not I will be fine." He leaned in for a pop kiss.

"Somehow this doesn't feel right," I couldn't ignore the awkward sensation deep within me.

After a few hours, Dion returned home. I sat in a daze contemplating the entire Kleon situation when Rodrigo broke my train of thought, "Kasey, we will be going down to the *hogueras*, around eleven o'clock. You might want to dress warm it will be a cold night. Mama and Papa said they have to pick up some wine. Would you mind driving us there?"

"No, *no problema. Gracias* Rodrigo."

The reports claimed Mallorca would experience record lows tonight. They believed that it might even drop into the low thirties. Being from such a warm state my bones and muscles reacted poorly to the cold weather. That night I put on my jeans, sneakers, my royal blue turtleneck sweater, and my black wool jacket. I even slipped on black gloves to make sure not a single part of me felt the cold.

We headed out late, closer to eleven thirty. We could see the light from deep within the dark forest. I figured that the bon fire must be massive in size. The blazes glowed from the path. Once we came to the clearing, it was a remarkable spectacle. In the middle of the site, a rim of small stones surrounded a dancing wild fire. In the far corner of the clearing, some local men with their classical guitars in hand played melodies with Flamenco rhythms. The villagers danced, sung, and drank wine.

The celebration honored the first night of winter and the air outside gave no mercy to that fact. Even with the fire, and the warm attire, the chill hit the core of every bone in my body. Off to the side I noticed a smaller bon fire with a line of people waiting to jump over it. Catalina laid out a blanket to sit on and the boys ran off dancing in the rotunda. I sat next to Catalina she smiled and gave me a nod. Fernando and Beatriz showed up with more cases of wine. They immediately went to mingle with their friends, but not before Fernando placed half a glass of red merlot in Catalina and my hand.

"It will keep you ladies warm," he said before joining his wife and their friends. The oaky wine slid down my throat with a heavy coating.

"Do you plan to jump tonight?" Catalina surprised me as she tried to start conversation.

"I don't know. It looks like fun. Why do they do it?"

"Health, for the long winter and the year to come. The celebration is an old tradition. It is a much bigger festival in other cities." Catalina put her wine glass down and stood. She extended her hand down towards me.

"Come, I will jump with you."

Seeing the perfect opportunity to mend my relationship with her, I put my glass down and reached out for her hand.

"Does it get hot?" We put ourselves in the fast moving line.

"It is fire, what do you think," she said in her Catalina way. The flames raised three feet off the ground. Two men stood on the other side with blankets ready to put out anyone who caught fire.

Our turn came up. She grabbed my hand, and hunched down ready to sprint. "Run as fast as you can, jump high enough to land on the other side," she laughed. Catalina, fun! Where did this come from? Finally, after all these months she opened up. Catalina started without any warning. We ran together holding hands. As soon as we hit the edge of the fire, we jumped. I brought my legs forward as I would in the long jump during gym class. The blaze prickled the bottom of my feet. My skewed perception, as we went over the fire, gave the impression that the flames rose with an attempt to catch us.

We passed through a fog of heat before we both landed on the other side laughing. The smoke I inhaled burned the insides of my nose. The smell of the burnt wood attached itself to my clothing.

"Thanks. That was fun." The warm air from my breath puffed out.

"You are welcome," she smiled.

A familiar old woman sat tapping her foot next to the men with guitars. Helen of Troy, sung along cheerful with a glass of wine in her hand.

"I'm going to see someone. I'll be there in a sec." I told Catalina.

I approached and knelt beside her cane starring in awe at the demi goddess before me. She smiled and wacked the side of my body with her cane.

"Hello, Kassandra." She spoke in English!

"How did you know it was me?"

"Your smell is unforgettable, same as the woman, whose lineage you carry." She added wrinkles to her cheeks with a smile. Gorgeous, even in her old age, she couldn't hide her beauty.

"I didn't know you can speak English. Why didn't you the day we met?"

What did she mean from the lineage I carry?

"Ah, that was your Dion's doing. He is the sneaky one, out of the brothers," she smirked. She placed her hand to my cheek. I froze my thoughts worrying about what I was thinking.

She laughed. "Do not worry so much young one. It is a waste to live life with worries. The lineage I speak of is the one you carry from Pandora."

"How is this possible?" I asked.

"This I do not know. Your existence puts to rest all the rumors that have circulated about her." She sipped her wine.

"What do you mean?"

"Pandora has not been seen for the past three thousand years. She allied with the other side and vanished. Rumor is, that if Zeus came back to Earth, he had a score to settle with her."

With vindication she smiled, "She betrayed them all. You are proof that she is still on Earth."

A chill trickled down my spine. The band started a new song and Helen joined in with her lyrical voice. I placed her hand in between mine and squeezed, "thank you."

I joined Catalina on the blanket.

"So, Kasey why is Dion not here?" Catalina asked.

"He's back home with his brothers." I watched my words. The mention of his name evoked feelings of anxiety. I sipped more wine.

"Does it have to do with James leaving?" She asked in a casual way.

"What do you mean?"

She looked at me bewildered. "You do not know?"

"What?" I asked.

"James said he was leaving tonight and he wanted to say good bye. He said it would only be for a few months then he would return."

I must have looked horrified because she asked, "What is wrong?"

What was James' plan? Was he a planted device to infiltrate the house? Could he really be that sneaky to his own brothers? All of a sudden anxious turned into panic. They were clueless as to what was coming to them. I have to get to them I must help.

"Tell your parents I went to see Dion." I put my wine glass down and ran. I sprinted as fast as I could down the dark path and straight to my car. I couldn't breathe. My lungs rejected the cold air. A simple ten-minute car ride felt like a never-ending journey. I didn't even bother knocking I approached their red door and entered the living room. Shadows stood outside in the pool deck area.

## 17. Dion vs. Sam

*Late that afternoon.

I left her house and found my brothers all minus James sitting in Max's room.

"What is going on?" I asked as I entered.

"We are discussing strategic plans. I wish to be prepared for anything," Max said acting as if he was going into battle.

"Look he came after Kasey. I will go for him first. He is mine." I owed it to her to make sure Sam got what was coming to him.

"Dion, we all want to assure Sam pays justly for what he did to Kasey. But you cannot think you are going to take him down single handedly," Max huffed at me.

"Where is James? Should he not be in here?" Martin asked.

"James, until recently was with Sam. I love my brother dearly, but I do not want to trust him, yet," Max said.

He continued. "Sam has an advantage over us. Even in his spirit state he can now make physical contact with the concrete world."

"Wait, since when could he affect the human world in his spirit form?" Antony asked.

"That is what James told me. He has spent many years evolving his ability and pushing the limit of what he can do further. He is able to harness his spirit form so that it actually can interact with the physical world as if he were a living being. Apparently in his spirit form he is also more powerful." Max looked at me concerned.

"I did not say anything because I knew you would explode with anger, Dion. But one of the things that upset James was, he is not entirely sure Sam did not push Kasey over the ledge purposely. James says that Sam at times, is uncontrollable in spirit form…"

I stood up and clenched my fist.

"Dion, revenge will only get you killed. James believes that when Sam is in his spirit form he is not himself anymore, he is out of control, violent. He can morph into anything. That day he was chasing Kasey as a tiger." Max informed.

"I do not know if I can keep control tonight!" I paced the floor.

"You are going to have to. We have to stick to the plan as best as possible," Max said annoyed.

"What is the plan, Max?" John stood and began to pace with me.

"John, Martin, I want you to stay behind James. Do not let him out of your sight. I want you to make a move on him before we give him the chance to move on us. Whether he is on our side or not." The twins nodded. "Now, gentlemen can you focus and give us any heads up about tonight?" Max asked them.

"We have been trying, nothing has come up yet," Martin said frustrated.

"Antony." Max looked at him.

Antony nodded. "I will have a talk with Layna, we will be ready."

"Good, because if we ever need to separate James and Sam she will be a great distraction." Max turned to me.

"You and I will go for Sam. I have a plan, I do not know if it will work but if it does, Sam will be caged for as long as we keep him that way."

"Now remember the curse. As long as he is chanting it, if he manages to stick a blade in us, we are done. Do not take James for granted either he is just as capable to use the curse for himself." Max looked at the twins, "protect yourselves and stay safe." Then he swallowed hard, "I do not want to lose any brothers here tonight. Now, go and do what you have to. Prepare for tonight. Stay behind Dion, I want to talk to you about what I have planned for Sam."

Max and I spent the next few hours going over our part of the plan. Antony had the task to prepare the weapon. At eleven thirty, Martin and John received a premonition. They came into the weapons room where Max, Antony, and I readied our swords.

"He is soon to be on his way," Martin said.

"It is going to happen on the pool deck. That is where I see us all being," John imputed.

"So it has begun." Max took a deep breath. I grabbed my Pugio Dagger. Squeezing the handle twice, I headed out the door. Max preferred the Roman Spatha, the twins took their Gladius swords, and Antony took his Moorish Scimitar. We chose not to carry shields. We never fought with them and thought they would slow us down. James joined us and picked out a Gladius for himself.

Camouflaged for the night in thin black sweaters and jeans, we positioned ourselves. The cold night air and the slight breeze sent chills that I ignored. We stood outside anticipating his arrival, Max in front, I to his right, Antony to his left with Layna at his side. Following behind, were James, Martin, and John. The tall grayish ghost figure approached through the forest pathway. Sam appeared in spirit form, a monstrous looking image of himself. His face contorted, wrinkled, and aged. He resembled a Hollywood ghoul. Sam stopped at the edge of the deck.

"Good evening brothers," he said in a hollow tone. His body nowhere in sight.

"Sam," Max replied.

"What shall it be Max, have you chosen to do the right thing and end this pathetic eternal suffrage?"

Max tensed and replied. "Sam, we told you once, nothing has changed. We have no plan to leave this world, not tonight."

"I see, seems like you boys were anticipating somewhat of a brawl." Sam pointed to the swords in our hands.

"We hope that this can be resolved amicably. What is this to you, why is it important?" Max negotiated.

"Nothing amicable about the sword in your hand brother," Sam snapped. "You always did feel like you knew what was best for the family. Well tonight, I am going to bring salvation to this family, and you will thank me Max when your spirit is once again with Cyra's. Let us say I am paying for an overdue debt."

Max and I leaned forward ready to charge. In unison we ran as Sam's ghost materialized a sword into his hand. Before his spirit-self approached us, it split into two identical selves. The fact that he could portray more than one spirit ghost at a time, was a new revelation. The metals of our swords silently struck each other with mighty force and the battle began.

I focused on the spirit to the left as Max battled the one on the right. Ahead of his every move, I moved from place to place ensuring that he did not land a swing. Our swords touched only when I commanded it, to change his direction or slow him down. From what I could tell, Max struggled with Sam's powerful swings. It almost seemed as if Sam focused his energy on Max.

They danced around with grace and brutal force as every swing swooshed through the quiet night air. The grunts from both men masked a thousand years of anger. Attempting to move Sam's spirit down toward the forest path, I lead him away from his other ghost half. Achieving my goal, I peered around at my surroundings to get accurate locations on everyone.

John and Martin yelled, "Antony he is on the roof."

I knew the Twins worked on getting a vision as to where Sam placed his dormant body. Antony and Layna headed for the roof.

James stopped them with his mind. "Are you searching for his body? I will bring him down."

From the corner of my eye, a shadowy physique lifted from the roof floating onto a lounge chair. Antony and Layna sneaked their way closer near Sam's body. Layna carried the special sword in her mouth. I knew my part was to keep Sam distracted long enough for Antony to stab Sam's lifeless frame with the sword. In the meantime, Sam the spirit guided Max closer to his dormant body. Antony pulled the sword with the chain straight towards Sam's body.

James yelled, "Noooo…that is not a fair fight."

James lifted Antony through the air and tossed him with force into the tall trees. Layna angered by James' action charged and attacked him with great brutality. She latched herself to his arm and knocked him down. He pulled her off throwing her into the pool. Sam's ghost not missing a beat continued to spar with diligence. The rapid clinging and clanking of swords striking resonated in the night. John and Martin moved on James. All of a sudden, the spirit I battled vanished in a puff of mist. My powerful swing sliced through the air at nothing. I turned my gaze to Max. In a fraction of a second, Sam's ghost vanished into his body and Sam arose. He placed his hand into his jacket and took out a blade. With exact precision, he inserted the metal into Max.

Sam held the handle and whispered, "I love you brother," then in Greek, he chanted.

> "And let it be upon this immortal,
> That was sentence by mighty wraths,
> To lay eternally in the heavens,
> By the steel of his kindred's blade,
> And to thy blades owner,
> May the Grace's gifts be now bestowed."

"NOOOOOOO," I screamed. Max fell over onto his side. Her high pitch cry echoed. Kasey appeared from the shadows of the house mortified.

"Antony!" I screamed as Sam picked up Max's sword and charged me. I moved fast down the path, my objective to get him away from the others. I did not stop to go down the stairs, I ran off the cliff. Soaring through the air, I managed to land on my feet. The roar of the rough sea hitting our rocky shore gave me the atmosphere I needed for my revenge.

Sam attempted to do the same but failed to land properly and fell on his side. It only took him an instant before he popped up, "Dion, think about what I am offering you. Do not pass this up because of a human."

"I have no idea who you are anymore Sam, clearly not a brother of ours."

My fingers tightened around the handle.

"I did not push her Dion. I tried to save her," he yelled.

"Save her! I saw her back Sam, what animal would do such a thing to save her. You cannot be trusted your words are lies!" I bent low and charged him. Overcome with an exuberant amount of rage I challenged him, "Man on man, no abilities."

"We fight raw then," he agreed.

With all the natural strength God gave me, I swung on him. We circled each other with mighty blows. As we got close to the shoreline, the chilly water splashed around creating droplets of water flying through the air. Then a hand full of Elenora's falcons flocked onto Sam and pecked at him. One of the birds flew at me with the special sword. Anthony created a sword with a chain and lock welded to its handle. Ignoring the falcons, I entered their black feathered cloud and plunged the blade into Sam's chest. With the chain in hand, I reached behind him and wrapped it around his back and chest. Then locked it to the handle, the sword then became a permanent fixture in Sam's body. He fell lifeless, onto the sand and ocean water. The birds flew away.

"Noooo! What are you doing to him?" James barreled through the night. He stood at the bottom of the staircase, along with Martin and Kasey. Antony stationed himself at the top of the cliff. I imagined John was with our beloved Max. James ran half way toward us and stopped.

"He is not dead James, simply contained," I barked.

"So, our creation worked." Max's loud voice came screaming from the top of the cliff. He and John appeared through the dark forest. His sweater slashed from where Sam's blade pierced through.

"The curse, it did not work?" James screamed up to Max.

"It must have been a fake, a ploy. James, it is over." Max smirked.

"You cannot keep Sam like that Dion, release him it is not right. He is our brother," James growled.

"Why not? Now he cannot hurt anyone else." I had no patience left for my little brother.

"He never intended to hurt anyone, let him go!" James commanded. Then he looked around, quicker than anyone could even see, he lifted two pieces of rope debris from the rocks and wrapped them tightly around Kasey's wrist and ankles.

"What are you doing?" she panicked.

I sprinted to her, but James' can move objects with his mind as fast as I can with my body. With a powerful force, he threw my body into the rocks. A moment of pain impaled my back. Within seconds, I was back on my feet in time to see Kasey's body lifted through the air. Martin lunged for her but missed. With a violent thrust, James tossed Martin back into the stairs. He dangled her body upside down over the turbulent waters. Her screams shrilled as she swayed.

"No one move or she falls," James ordered. I froze as well did everyone else.

"Let go of her James." It took everything within my power to remain calm.

"Un-do the sword in Sam's chest, now!" He screamed. "I do not want to hurt her, but you cannot do this to Sam."

"Dion, do as he says," Max yelled.

Antony took the key to the lock off his neck and handed it to Layna. She came down the steps missing two or three at a time. I bent over Sam's lifeless body. Layna strutted to me with the chain in her mouth that held the key. She placed it in my hand. I unlocked the chain, then drew the sword from Sam's chest. His spirit form rose in a cloud of grey smoke. He smelled like death. Angry, he swung at me. I threw the sword with the chain into the rocky beach and with my Pugio Dagger began to spar with Sam once more.

Martin pointed his sword onto James and moved on him. He turned to strike Martin. Her shriek caused everyone to freeze. We watched as her body hit the cold water. Kasey disappeared into the dark her body did not resurface. Martin shoved James aside and ran to the shoreline. He removed his shirt and shoes and dove in. Sam not allowing Kasey to be a distraction for me continued to exchange blows.

John scream, "James what have you done!"

My brothers ran down the wooden staircase toward the beach.

As Sam and I got away from the shoreline, his lifeless body began to lift through the air. It spun round and round gliding away from me. He flew spiraling through the sky down the beach.

Sam's spirit ghost yelled, "Nooo, James!" But James ran with Sam's body out of the scene. The minute the two were out of sight Sam's spirit vanished into the air.

I stepped out into the shallow waters of the ocean and exhaled a deep breath of cold air when Martin surfaced with his arms around Kasey both swimming to shore. I ran and met them a few feet from the shore's edge. She coughed, but otherwise all right. I placed my arm around her waist and helped her to shore. She collapsed onto her back on the sand attempting to catch her breath.

"Are you alright?" I asked leaning over her.

Gasping and with a quivering bottom lip she replied, "CCCold."

I helped her up and we headed toward the top of the cliff. I put an arm under her shoulders, her coat felt like it was a sponge of cold water. She stunk like burnt wood.

"Should we go after him?" I asked Max when we reached the top.

"I think it is over. He will not be back. Take her inside and get her warm," Max ordered.

I headed for the house. Her lips trembled and she shivered. Once inside I grabbed her cold hand and led her to my room and into the bathroom. I turned the faucet to the tub and began filling it with warm water. Overwhelmed with an aggressive adrenaline from the fight, I could not believe she disregarded my orders. Harsh, I unbuttoned her coat and pulled it off.

She managed to stutter, "DDiion!"

"Kasey, you have to get out of these cloths. It is too cold, look at you. You need to get in the warm bath. I do not want you sick," I said annoyed with her disobedience tonight.

She nodded, and began to remove her gloves, shoes, and socks. The cold droplets of water ran down from the tips of her hair. With shaking hands, she unbuttoned her jeans and began to pull them down.

Did she want me to leave? Should I stay? I lowered my eyes away as soon as I caught a glimpse of her orange and red string underwear. She had not made it past her lower hips when we heard a knock on the bedroom door.

She stopped, her eyes bulged out.

"Relax, I shall see who it is," I said.

I took a deep breath and opened the door.

"How is she? Is she alright?" Max asked concerned.

"Yes, she is getting into warm water as we speak." All the muscles in my face were tense from the night's activities.

Max noticed my demeanor. "Good. That is good for her. Dion we did well tonight." He shook his head.

I let out a heavy breath.

"Dion relax. They are gone and I do not think they will be coming back, not any time soon." He stepped closer forcing eye contact. "I know... I know you are disappointed with how your brothers have acted. Perhaps one day we seven can stand side by side on good terms, but for now focus on taking care of her. I brought both of you some Volteo from the Rioja region. It will warm her." He handed me two glasses filled with the red wine. I gave him a brotherly hug.

I returned to the bathroom door and knocked.

"Come in," she said. I inched the door open a crack not peering in.

"Are you sure?" I asked uncertain if I should see her naked.

"Yes, it's fine."

I opened the door, walked in, and closed it behind me to keep the steam in. Her silhouette figure sat behind the curtain in the tub. Her bright smiling head peeked out from behind the curtain. She had stopped shaking and looked more relaxed. Her lower lip would quiver from time to time.

"Who was that," she asked.

"Max, he brought you some medicine." I handed her the glass of wine.

"Oh, he's such a good Doctor." She held the curtain in place with one hand as she reached out and took the glass with the other. She took a small sip. I rubbed my eyes together, sat on the toilet lid, and took a big sip.

"Are you okay Dion?" she worried.

"It has been a long night," I looked away.

"Yes, it has," she replied somber. "Do you think they will be back?"

"We do not think so, but with those two who knows." I continued my discontent attitude toward her.

"Are you angry with me?" she asked sweet.

I looked right at her. "I am absolutely furious with you."

Her mouth dropped and her eyes grew big. I closed my eyes and took a slow sip of wine.

My words were too harsh. "I am sorry I do not mean to be so unkind." I drank more wine.

Kasey gave me an attempt at a smile then looked down at her body. "Why is it that I always end up naked when I'm around you?" she asked in a tease attempting to soften me up.

"That is because you cannot follow directions," I said stern.

"I'm sorry Dion, Catalina told me that James planned to go away and I thought he was betraying you guys. So I came to warn you." She avoided eye contact.

"Kasey, do you not realize that something could have happened to you tonight. What would I have done if I had lost you out there?" I knelt down beside the tub. "You have no idea how delicate you are."

"I'm sorry," she said looking like a sweet soaked seal. "I might not be unstoppable or have super powers, but I'm not fragile just cause I'm human. You treat me like I could break to pieces at any minute."

"You can your human. Look at what happened out there, you could have drowned. You would be dead if Max did not put your spine back together. How can you be so reckless with your life?"

"It is my life. I'm being human. I'm part of your immortal world now, whether you like it or not and you can't keep me in a safe bubble."

"Kase, I cannot lose you yet, I just got you. I know that day will come, you have a right to die, but I would not be able to handle it if it happens now."

She swallowed, "I'm sorry, I didn't mean to upset you."

I leaned in and kissed her.

"Oh, my love, your lips are still so cold." I backed off.

I sat on the toilet lid, and took a few more sips of wine so did she. I relaxed my shoulders.

"By the way, you know who we heard from today? Professor Darius Mubarak."

She swallowed hard. "I know, I'm related to Pandora."

Taken by surprise I asked, "How...?"

"I spoke to Helen at the *hogueras*, she too mentioned my lineage to Pandora. What did the Professor say?"

"He said it is scary how similar your DNA is to Pandora's. She must be no more than three generations from you."

"How is that possible? I thought immortals could not breed anymore," she asked.

"We cannot. I do not know, perhaps we need to look into your lineage and see how many of Pandora's descendants there are."

"Yeah, something." She shook her head and shrugged her shoulders. She pulled the curtain back her silhouette lean down and dipped into the water. Overheated, I tugged at my thin knitted sweater. I took another sip of wine. She ran her hands through her hair and I swallowed nervous. I wanted her. I wanted to see the natural beauty that lay behind that curtain. She popped her head back out.

"Are you all right?" she asked bewildered.

"I think I am going to have to remove myself from the bathroom soon."

It took her a second to grasp my subtleness. With a grin, she looked down at her naked body.

"Ah, I understand," she said. If her cheeks were not already rosy pink, she would be blushing. I let out a long low breath, knelt down in front of the tub, and leaned in to kiss her. Her lips warmed up. The wetness from her soft skin left my own damp. As we kissed, I opened my eyes briefly. Her bare back, hip, thigh, and bent leg twisted forward in the water. Abruptly, I backed away.

I scooped up her dripping, burnt smelling, clothes from the bathroom floor.

"What are you doing," she asked with some worry.

"I am taking them to the dryer. I most certainly am not sending you home to the Castillo's in my clothes again," I smiled at her and made a quick exit from the bathroom.

## 18. Kasey's Spanish Christmas

December 24th the busiest I have ever been in Deia. The preparations for the night's festivities took days. I spent the entire day helping in the kitchen. The feast that was prepared for after the midnight mass was enormous in quantity. These new experiences were something I relished. I even looked forward to the Mass until one in the morning and then the party until the early morning hours. What a way to enter Christmas day partying all night.

The wine drinking started early afternoon on Christmas Eve and went well until sundown Christmas day. I was to meet Dion at his house before the mass then we would ride together to church. The Castillo's had to be there earlier because Garcia and Rodrigo sang in the all boys choir. The temperature was pleasant, warmer than the night of the winter solstice. I put on a fuzzy, vibrant, green, and silver thin turtleneck sweater with a long flowing white skirt and my white boots. I styled my hair half way up.

The Kleon house bustled with five men trying to get ready, tying ties, finding shoes, and a very potent smell of different kinds of after shaves. The mood at the house for the past few days had been a somber one. Even though they were coming out and celebrating tonight the truth was that, they were still hurt and bothered by the actions of Sam and James. Yet with everything that happened, they yearn for the family to be complete again.

I walked in with the bag of presents in hand. John and Martin stood in the living room. Martin tied John's bow tie. They were both in slick black suits with red shirts. No one would be able to tell them apart aside for the fact that Martin had a black tie and John a bow tie.

"*Feliz Navidad*, Kasey," they said in unison giving me kisses on my cheeks.

"Merry Christmas to you as well." I gave them hugs.

"Oohh, are those presents for us?" John eyed the bag.

"Yes, but not until Christmas." I took them away and placed them on the coffee table. Due to the hectic past week, the boys never decorated for the season.

John closed his eyes and put his hand over them as if he either had a headache, or was concentrating.

He opened his eyes and said, "Thanks Kase I love it." Then he kissed my cheek.

My jaw dropped, "Did you really just see what was in the bag?" I asked annoyed.

"No, he does not know. He is fooling with you Kasey." Martin turned his brother in.

"Yeah, Martin will not let me see what you got us. We have to focus on it together or we get nothing. He has been blocking it since we heard you bought us gifts," John sat on the couch sulky.

"Don't get too excited about it John. You guys have everything imaginable. This is a little something. Not a big deal."

"I know Kasey, but because we have everything we need, we stopped giving each other gifts a few centuries ago. I think it was nice that you got us a gift," John said sincere.

"It is a gracious act. You really did not need to." Max entered the conversation stepping into view at the top of the stairs. He is truly a handsome man. Especially in a black and white, tie tuxedo.

He gave me a smile and greeted me with a kiss as he stepped into the foyer.

"Everyone looks great tonight," I said. They looked classic, aristocratic.

Layna entered the room from the kitchen wearing a big red bow. She walked up to me and I held my breath. Even though she was friendly, I still had my reservations about such a wild cat. She placed her head under my hand and I rubbed her ears.

"She wishes you a Merry Christmas," Antony said coming down from the stairs. He cleaned up. He had on a black suit with an opened jacket. His white shirt had the two top buttons undone. We greeted each other.

Then he appeared at the top of the stairs. I let out a soft gasp. He was magnificent in his black on black suit and red tie. The epitome of perfection. In his James Bond way, he strolled down the stairs. He placed his hands on my waist.

"You look amazing," I whispered.

His smile melted my heart, "Not nearly as enchanting as you."

We greeted each other with a soft kiss. His brothers turned and looked away to give us our moment.

"I have never seen your eyes as vibrant as they are tonight," he said. I gave him an Eskimo kiss.

"All right you two, let us get a picture. So we can all say in five years how Dion looks exactly the same," John took out a camera.

The comment was odd but I didn't want to think about anything like that, not tonight. Dion and I posed for the picture and John took it saying, "Good looking couple."

"All right let us go," Max cut him off.

Dion and I rode together to the church. There were masses of people walking down the cobblestoned road heading up the hill to the church.

"Kasey have you ever been to a Christmas Eve service?" Dion asked. I gave him a look that suggested he rethink his question.

He smiled and nodded. "You know even if a person is not of the faith I believe it is something everyone should experience for the mere fact that it is positively memorable."

We entered the church and seating was rare to find. Most of the men were standing while they allowed the women to sit. There was a spot for one more in the very last pew, he gestured for me to take it.

Shaking my head no I said, "I don't mind standing."

He leaned up against the church's sand stonewall and I leaned against his chest. Then he wrapped his arms around my waist. The aroma of fresh greenery from the natural wreaths and garland filled the church. Everything was lit by candlelight. The flutist, violinist, and organist played as the angelic voices of the boys' choir echoed. I was familiar with a few of the songs solely based on their melodies. Everything in Spanish, I couldn't make out the lyrics.

I'm not sure if it was because the atmosphere enhanced the experience, but the songs that I have known all my life listening to them on the Christmas radio station seem to have a mesmerizing affect within the walls of the church. It didn't matter that I couldn't understand a word, the music, the story, and the whole town of Deia made the experience tender. By the end of the service, emotional, I wiped my glossed eyes. Dion squeezed me tight.

After the midnight mass, we headed for the feast. The Castillo's turned the restaurant into a great party hall. We set up two rows of tables all along the walls. The middle was open for the dancing. Then a beautiful buffet table, sat on the back wall, with its own schedule for the night.

First, they would bring out appetizers of hams, *chorizos*, and cheeses. Then the first course, a fish soup. After the soup the main course, roast lamb. Following the main course, an assortment of desserts laid out. The entire place filled up with approximately eighty of the jolliest people drinking wine, eating, and laughing with good friends.

Fernando along with some of his male friends and family members brought out the guitars and began to play. The floor filled with people dancing. Even Martin sat down with the men and pick up a guitar. Dion and I danced and drank all night. John stepped up and reluctantly asked Catalina to dance. She missed James.

I would treasure this life experience for as long as I lived. Around four in the morning, the place settled down. Gently, I let Fernando and Beatriz know that I was going to hang out at Dion's the rest of the morning. They understood and accepted. I think all the wine they had drunk helped my case.

Either way, after helping clean up I headed back with Dion. We arrived at the house before his brothers.

"I am glad they are not here yet," Dion said as we walked through the door. "I wanted to have some private time with you."

"Oh, what did you want to do with the private time," I asked suggestive. I grabbed his tie and pulled him in for a kiss.

"There is time for that later," he smiled. "I wanted to give you your Christmas present."

"Okay, let me grab yours." I rummaged through my bags of presents.

"Let us go out to the pool deck. In case, they come home. We will not be bothered out there." He took my hand and led me out to the pool. He acted funny and stressed the private time. I began to let my crazy thoughts get the better of me. Why would he want to have the perfect private ambiance unless he was going to … Oh, God I thought, please don't let him propose to me! By the time, we got out to the pool deck I was in an internal panic.

We sat down at the round wooden table. I couldn't look at him.

"Kasey, is everything all right?"

I nodded, but said nothing.

"Would you like me to go first?" he asked unsure.

"Yes, please open yours first." I passed him a big box and then a smaller one.

"Two presents! You out did yourself," he smiled then began to unwrap the larger present. The orange hues of sunrise started to form on the crest of the Mediterranean Sea.

He undid the lid on the bigger box and began to laugh. "You got me running shoes!"

"I was told that they are the best out there for sprinting." I laughed with him.

"That is great." Then he proceeded to open the smaller box.

Anxious I stopped him. "Wait!" I said nervous. "I..." I swallowed hard, "It's just..."

"Kasey, what is it?" he asked.

"Please tell me you aren't going to propose to me." I held my breath.

He froze and looked stunned. "Well obviously not anymore," he said sarcastic. My eyes shot open in horror.

He bit his upper lip trying not to laugh. "That was mean of me, sorry Kasey. I could not help myself. No, I was not planning on proposing to you tonight."

I let out a huge sigh, "Oh, Dion that was not funny."

He lost it and laughed.

He reached over and caressed my cheek. "Kasey...there is nothing I would love more than for you to be my wife one day. I do not think that time is yet."

"Oh, no, Dion, I completely agree. It was just the whole set up I...I am over analytical sometimes."

"Most of the time actually." He removed his hand. "Can I open this now?" he asked.

"Yes, but don't..." I started to say.

"Kasey, you are doing it again. Let me make up my own mind about it."

I let out a big sigh, "Okay, open it."

He began to un-wrap the small box. It was one of the glass Christmas ornaments with a wooden carving inside. The carving was the Irish trinity knot interwoven around an Irish Claddagh.

He grinned, "Hmm...the symbol of spiritual growth, eternal life, and undying love."

I blushed. He took my hand and butterfly kissed the back of it.

"It is not too much and not too little. It is perfect my love," he said. I blushed further giving him a radiant smile.

"Now for my gift," he said excited.

"Yes," I joined his enthusiasm. "Now that I know it is not a..."

He pulled out a ring box and set it on the table. My smile turned to a frown.

"Dion, what's this?" I said harsh.

He smirked and shrugged his shoulders.

"Oh, you wouldn't? Would you?" I asked not knowing if he was pulling my chain again or not.

"Open it and you shall find out," he said.

I took the little black box and creaked it open. A key sized pendant illuminated like a torch. With a ruby rose and emerald leaves resting on the hilt of a golden sword. The rose's stem coiled tightly down the silver blade.

"Oh, Dion," I whispered.

"It belonged to Catherine the Great. I thought it matched your red hair and green eyes perfectly. It is something we acquired some time ago. I bought the necklace so that you could wear it around your neck," he said pulling out a necklace from inside his coat.

"I can't take this," I whispered.

"Do you not like it?" he asked taking it out of the box and sliding it on the white gold necklace.

"Dion, it belonged to a prominent Russian empress. I can't wear this around my neck. It's value alone."

"Do not worry about what it is worth." He stood and walked behind me. Dion placed it on my neck. It radiated against my green sweater. I inhaled feeling the weight of the treasure on my chest. It was delicate, womanly, and amazing.

"Did I choose wrong do you not like it?" he asked as he sat back down.

I looked down at the remarkable charm. "It's not too much, and it's not too little. It's perfect," I smiled.

He placed his hand under my ear and held my cheek in his palm. Then we both leaned into each other and with a gentle embrace, we kissed. We stayed this way for what seemed too short of a time. I held his hand and rubbed my thumb on the inside of his palm.

"Dion," I said as we sat with our foreheads pressed together. "I want to find Pandora. Would you help me?"

He took his head back, "Yes."

Here's a sneak peek at

Book Two
Jar of Pandora

Coming in 2012

# 1
## Kasey Farewell Spain

My fingers squeezed his hand. The takeoff always made me queasy. An hour earlier, I loaded myself with various drugs from motion sickness to nausea reducers. I shook my foot, closed my eyes, and tried to remember to breathe.

"How ever did you do this all alone when you came to Spain?" Dion asked me.

"Same. I held my breath and closed my eyes. I tried focusing on some music," I said keeping my eyes shut and my head pressed against the first class seat cushion.

"It will be all right. We are soon to take off and then we shall be in the air. Is it take off or the entire plane ride that makes you ill?" he asked concerned.

"Takeoff and landing." I wished he'd stop asking questions.

"Well, then good, it will soon be over." Dion held my hand for reassurance.

"Is she all right, she looks ill? Can I help?" Max asked. I opened my eyes and he was leaning over us.

"Thank you but I do not think you can cure fear," Dion smiled at his older brother who has the ability to heal with his touch.

Max gave me a sympathetic look, "It will soon be over Kasey. Remember take deep breaths." He went back to his seat.

After the holidays, my second semester of high school in Mallorca, Spain was busy. Dion and I had grown close and unequivocally inseparable. With his ability for speed, he ran me to Barcelona and we spent a weekend sightseeing. Spain seemed like a dream.

Other than the fact that I wanted to see my brother and family, Deia, Spain marked itself as a place with a thousand memories for me. I stole the best part of my trip, Dion.

The low vibrations of the plane intensified as we accelerated down the runway. I remembered slow steady breaths. The slight pressure pressed me back into my seat. Then the plane lifted and my stomach ascended. That is the sensation that makes me sick.

"Kasey, your color, you are turning green, are you breathing?" Dion sounded worried.

Once the plane stabilized, I relaxed. I opened my eyes and took in a few deep breaths.

"I have never seen someone's skin turn that shade before. Quite impressive. I thought you would be sick for sure," he said shocked.

"That's why I skipped breakfast this morning and took all those meds." I let go of his hand and stretched.

"Do you require anything?" he asked.

"Water, I could use some water."

He motioned for the flight attendant. I grabbed one of those traveling pillows and laid it across Dion's shoulder. Then I nestled myself into it. He lifted his arm and held me close. Our attendant came over. Dion asked for some water and a soda for himself then she went to get it. The seat belt light flashed off. John popped his head in our personal seating space. John and Martin, Dion's twin younger brothers sat behind us.

"Hi," John smiled.

"Yes, how can we assist you?" Dion asked.

"Well, actually I wanted to suggest something to Kasey," he smiled amused.

I met his gaze. "Yes."

"You know Martin and I were thinking sometime in this ten hour flight you might want to tell Dion about your parents. I do not think the surprise factor would go over well in this situation. Just food for thought." Then he sat back down next to Martin.

I gasped. Dion looked confused.

"You know out of all the people to get the gift of past, present, and future, I wonder if it was such a good idea giving it to two fifteen year olds," I said loud enough so that they could hear. John gave my chair an abrupt kick. I sat up from the pillow and ran my hands through my hair. Panicked at what they must have seen. With their ability to see the future, past, and present nothing was a secret around them.

"Kasey is something wrong with your parents? Will they not like me?" Dion asked alarmed.

"Oh, no it's not that. No offense to you but they won't care one way or the other who you are. They always were open to us being with whomever we wanted."

"Then what is it?"

"Well, it's really bizarre. You must realize that when I told you my parents were free spirits, I didn't mean that lightly. Frankie and Sue are as free as birds in the sky." I tried to stress the issue.

"I understand," he chuckled. "Kasey, I have met all sorts of people from all sorts of walks of life throughout time, remember I am a two thousand year old saint. Nothing shocks me." He assured with confidence.

"Dion, I doubt you have ever met people like this."

"Kasey relax, it is going to be fine," he had no idea.

"Dion my parents are nudist and live in a nudist colony," I blurted out. His face froze his jaw dropped.

"Wait …what?" he stuttered confused and amused at the same time.

"They live naked," I replied sully.

"No…really." He pressed his lips together attempting to contain his laughter.

"Yes," I began to worry.

Then his face went from amused to uncertain. "Were you raised in a nudist colony?"

"No! No, no they moved into the colony while I was in Spain. This is their most recent crazy fad. I'm hoping it's a phase."

He placed his hand over his heart and let out the biggest laugh.

"So, when they pick us up from the airport…"

I interrupted, "They will be clothed. They only live in a compound where they can be naked, but only within the walls of that compound. That's why my brother hasn't been living with them, they chose to live this life style about eight months ago." I explained.

He starred straight into the seat in front of him.

"I'm so sorry and so embarrassed," I muttered.

"It will be alright," he smiled amused, "we do not choose our parents. So, are you staying with them and will you be naked too? Will I have to get naked, myself?" His lips widened his eyes unsure.

"No, people have a choice to be naked or to stay clothed, especially guests. As far as me staying there I was hoping I could stay in your house."

"You never have to ask you are always welcome," he said.

"That's one of the issues I have to work out as soon as I get back to St. Cloud. I figure I'm going to have to get a place so that Nolan has a proper home. Now, he's staying with..." I swallowed and decided to end my words there. I didn't need to get into details about my little brother living with my ex-fiancé.

"We have time to figure it all out," he said taking hold of my hand. Then his face went dead serious. He unbuckled himself, turned around in his seat so that his knees were on the seat cushion. He faced the twins, pointed a figure at them, and whispered sternly, "Not a word to anyone you understand!" He looked like a father scolding little children. Blatant laughter came from behind us.

I don't know what made me more ill. The landing or the fact that in a few minutes my family was going to meet Dion's family. After we landed, we passed through airport security easily. All we carried were duffel bags. Dion and his brothers shipped most of their possessions a week ago to their other brother Antony.

Antony having the ability to speak to animals left with his black panther, Layna a few months ago and purchased a home in St. Cloud, Florida. They shipped my one big suitcase.

My stomach sank the minute we came around the corner and approached the area where family members waited to pick up loved ones.

I saw Teal, my ex-fiancé with his perfect light tan skin, curly dirty blonde hair, band t-shirt, and board shorts. He stood with an assortment of balloons from 'I love you' to 'welcome home', and a small pot of dandelions. Nolan stood next to him anxiously looking out. My parents were nowhere in sight. They spotted me and both their faces lit up. Neither one would have guessed that the entourage of young men walking behind me, was not in fact random passengers heading in the same direction, but were with me.

# Why Read?
## By Marisette Burgess

As a teacher, I always began my first day of school with the same icebreaker. I would write two lies and a truth on the board about myself. It would look something like this:

> Went to France over the summer.
> Had to repeat the first grade.
> Am an expert water skier.

The kids would then have to figure out which one was true. Every year I conducted the same experiment and every year I received the same results. The kids were never right.

The truth is I repeated the first grade. I couldn't read, didn't like it, and wouldn't do it. How does a person who wouldn't and couldn't read end up becoming an author?

Here's how:

For many years, I spent my school days in the lowest reading group, with long hours of make-up work, and having to do summer school. Then around fourth grade, I picked up a chapter book. Little did I know that that one chapter book would change my life forever? It was the first Nancy Drew novel. I sat there and gave it my best shot.

Ask yourself this, what is the one thing about mystery books that gets people hooked into them?

The answer is simple, you have to finish the book to find out who committed the crime. Mystery books are hard to put down simply because we want to figure out the mystery. That was it my friends, I was hooked. I started to read Nancy Drew books one after another. Before I knew it, I was reading a chapter book or two a week!

Unbelievable! All of a sudden by the time I reached fifth grade I went from the bottom-reading group to the highest. Yes, it is true. There was no miracle or magic at work here, simply the power of books. My world changed dramatically, school was easy, A's were flowing in, and everyone was happy.

Then one day, around February of the fifth grade, I finished another mystery book and thought, "I can do this. It's not that hard."

And that was the first story I ever wrote. A mystery on Valentines. Once I finished the short story, I handed it to my first fan, my mother. I remember still to this day the minute she finished the story. The priceless look of shock on her face as she uttered the words, "Oh, you have talent."

I don't believe people are born able to walk we have to learn to do it. Same as intelligence, you can get smart. I would have never known I had a natural ability to spin words into stories if I hadn't read those books in the first place.

My success in my academics didn't stop with just the high reading group. I went further. By middle school, I was a swift composer of words. In the sixth grade, I wrote a two-page essay that paid me my first wage as a writer, two thousand dollars. After winning this prestigious award, my seventh grade English teacher asked if she could read my short novella. Proud of this fifty-page medieval love story, I more than eagerly handed it over to her. I recall that English class when she gave the whole class seatwork so that she could sit there in front of us and read the story. She sighed and giggled through parts. Everyone glanced at me, and beamed. She was utterly in awe. The story must have left an impression because the next thing I knew they were testing me for gifted.

Me, gifted? Not a chance! I was the kid who was the oldest in the class because I repeated first grade. I had been in the lowest reading groups and had to do summer school. Me...Gifted. How?

The answer is simple, I read myself smart. Yes, I passed that gifted test and went from the lowest of lows to the highest you could go.

Books changed my academic life. I went on to college and attained an English degree in writing from the University of Central Florida. I became a teacher enjoying every day when I hooked kids into books. Now I'm an author hoping that my books one day could do the same for a child who hasn't felt the power of the hook, yet.

Why read you ask, because it's simple, it can change your life!

Marisette Burgess is available for book events, guest speaking, and author interviews.

To contact Marisette go to
Marisetteburgess.com
Or
marisetteb@aol.com

CPSIA information can be obtained at www.ICGtesting.com
Printed in the USA
LVOW061548240512

283130LV00002B/4/P